The Witch of Land and Sea

by

Moira Cormack

MORTON & SMITH

Published by
Morton & Smith
23 Rostrevor Road
Stockport, Cheshire, SK3 8LQ

Paperback Edition 2016
ISBN 978-1-911484-01-1

Typeset by Mach 3 Solutions Ltd (www.mach3solutions.co.uk)
Printed and bound in Great Britain by T J International, Padstow

With thanks
to Lydia for your help and support,
and to Claire.

29/10/16

To Islay

Happy Reading

Maria
X

Acknowledgements

My thanks, as always, go to my friends and children for all their love, support, and tireless encouragement.

I am grateful to my writers group for all their kindness and gentle criticism during the writing of this book. Special thanks go to Claire Steele, who got me going in the first place, Jean Durrand, for her guidance throughout the process, Valerie Hardie, for her illustrations and laughs along the way, and lastly to my Publisher, Editor, and friend, Sarah Hutchinson. Thank you.

Prologue

The thief lurked in the shadows. Watching while the last bag was slung over a shoulder and the final shout of "Bye" had faded. Waiting until even the oldest, silent one had moved away to start her day. Still the thief remained hidden, feeling for the right moment. Her heart's desire, the thing she coveted most, was locked in an enormous clamshell. Since being adopted by the Healer she had seen it open again and again. The Healer would tap it three times and mutter an incantation under her breath. The thief was gifted in all the underhand ways and had leant her ears inwards, concentrating her whole being on those words. They had become a ritual for her and she repeated them now in an endless circle in her head. The shape of the words sat oddly in her mind and in her mouth but she had learnt them nonetheless.

Every tiny hair on her body was alive to the possibility of the theft and her fingers itched with promise. Her only movement was the flexing and relaxing of her digits. Still she lingered. Shapes flickered around her but no one came.

"Ghosts," she decided.

Quiet descended, lying heavily until the thief felt her time had come. Breaking from her hiding place, she made for the shell. Three gentle taps, mutter, mutter, then a seemingly infinite age before the clam jerked open. She grabbed the narwhal horn handle brush and reached for the mirror when the shell snapped shut. The high-pitched scream of a narwhal in pain broke the thief's trance and vibrated around the briny deep.

Cursing foully, she was off. Her tail powered her forwards through the ocean's depths. Fury engulfed her. They would not catch her and take away her prize. She had coveted it and stolen it, and now it was hers. Away, away she raced from the mer colony. So lost had she been in her desire that she had not considered being caught. To begin with, the din made by the wailing brush blocked out everything else. Slowly, she became aware of a calamitous noise growing behind her, at first confused and then focused. The chase was on.

They were coming after her; a fleeting glance showed her that they were not yet in sight. Her effort was so tremendous that her heart pounded in her chest.

"On, on," she told herself.

In front of her, the doom-laden bay materialised. Instinct, self-preservation must have brought her here. Nobody came to this place; the entrance was narrow and the current fierce, even for the mer. Another backwards glance revealed a mass of angry faces with gritted teeth and hair pulled hard back by their speed. Feeling their rage burning the tip of her tail, eating her choices, she swiftly drove herself onwards. Their battle cry echoed thunderously in the deep but she wasn't afraid of them. Hatred had isolated her from all her kind, except the Healer. As she scooted towards the bay, the Healer's face rose in her mind. Intelligent, generous, and unafraid, the Healer had taken her in and offered her a home. The love had been tempting until her craving for the brush and mirror, a unique gift from the narwhal, ruled her. Now she had one. At last, she had power. What did she care about anything, now the treasure was hers? Scorn for the Healer and the rest of the mer filled her in one quick flick of her tail.

The tide was on its way out fast and with the massive force of her willpower, she gave a last spurt of energy. She had escaped. The sound of the hue and cry dropped away. She relaxed. Too late! So busy had she been looking behind that she had failed to look ahead. A huge wave took her and smacked her hard against the sand. Then it sucked itself back into the breakers and was gone, leaving her high and dry.

Chapter 1

Ruby took a furtive look around her before she entered the bay. She wanted to make sure that she was all by herself. The day had fully risen so she needed to be careful. It seemed deserted so she decided to be brave and sit out in the open on a promontory.

There she perched on the edge of a black rock and gazed gloomily at the lapping waves, ignoring the noisy mewing of the gulls overhead. The tide was on its way out as she peered into a nearby rock pool. She dipped a finger in to stir things up. The movement startled a hermit crab which retreated into its shell, and some tiny, silver fish darted about in confusion at the intruder. She couldn't imagine ever growing bored of the rock pools. Each time the sea drew back, a new, small world was exposed for her enjoyment.

She was utterly fed up. School, her brother, the rest of her family, she didn't remember when it had all become so complicated. She never knew anymore if she would fit in from one day to the next. She longed for the normal days when she didn't say or do something clumsy. She remembered times when it hadn't been like this but it was now. Whatever she did felt wrong and she didn't understand why. So she had come here to escape from everyone and just be herself. She gave a deep sigh as she thought of her morning.

"Please let today be normal. Please let today be normal," Ruby had whispered to herself as she made her way to school.

She half dragged her bag behind her, bumping it along in an attempt to appear casual while she kept her eyes peeled for the other girls.

If they were in a pack, she was doomed but if Erin or Sophie were on their own then they would link up with her. Both girls were similar to her; not popular but not total losers either. Getting to school without being part of a group was a BIG 'no no.' Straight away, it made you look as if nobody liked you. The packs would close ranks, none of them wanting to be contaminated by you so you had to stand there all alone. Ruby cringed with horror to think about it. Sometimes, she would be enveloped into the pack and at other times left out in the cold. The scary bit was not knowing what each day would bring.

Ruby spotted Erin up ahead.

"Hey there, Erin, wait up," she said.

As Erin turned and waited, Ruby felt a little flicker of hope rise up inside her. Maybe, just maybe, the day was going to be fine. But then Mia had taken Erin's arm and Ruby had heard her say, "Oh, don't talk to her, Erin," and Erin hadn't. Tears pricked the back of her eyes but Ruby held her head high and stared fixedly at a space to one side of the two girls.

Life wasn't much easier at home, either. Her brother, Eric, was impossible and *so* bossy. Two years older and he lorded it over her, telling her what to do all the time. It had become worse over the last few months since he started High School. She remained at Primary but Ruby knew that didn't mean he was better than she was. They fought and bickered until her mum became cross or, even worse, sad. Now and again, she glimpsed the brother he used to be, like when the girls had picked on her for having freckles and he had strolled over, all big brother, and shooed them away. Sometimes, it felt as if he thought he was the only one allowed to boss her about! Really, it was maddening. She would show him. He'd told her never to come into this bay as it was dangerous, and waved his hands in front of her face going, "Waa, woo". He wanted to scare her. Well, it hadn't worked and she'd chosen this place despite his warnings. It seemed to her nowhere else offered her the same escape from him and those 'know-it-all' girls.

So here she was in the haunted bay. Her journey in had been far easier than she expected, as the sea was rarely this calm. Anger and frustration had driven her to this cove and kept her fear away. Running her fingers through her hair, they got stuck in a mass of knots so she decided to comb it. Even her hair was 'wrong'. Come to think of it, there wasn't much that wasn't irksome to her today. The other girls in her class spent hours combing their locks, chatting and laughing while they did it. Ruby wasn't convinced she was that type of girl; she liked swimming and exploring rocks, and finding crabs and other sea creatures. Her mane was normally a tangled mess that her mother complained was turning into dreadlocks. She took out her comb and her sea-green mirror and started to tug at her hair.

She loved her mirror; it had belonged to her Nan and she kept it with her all the time. Most unusually, its handle had been carved from a narwhal's horn. The sea unicorn's horn could only be

11

given as a gift and there were some strange rumours about how it had come into her Nan's family. Ruby thought that they only made her Nan more intriguing, if that was possible. She had a rough little bag that she hid it in. Whenever the other girls asked what was in it, she would pull out a sea snake or a batfish – boy, were they ugly – and that stopped them asking.

Her reflection showed a turned-up, freckled nose, smallish eyes (certainly not big), pale lashes, and a sulky expression. She stuck her tongue out at it and suddenly laughed. As she did so, she hit a barnacle.

"Oww. I wish I didn't have a stupid tail!" she said, aloud.

She bent down to rub the sore bit and gave a double take. Her tail had gone. All her other worries dissolved as she stared at her legs.

Chapter 2

Legs? Her legs? She couldn't take it in. She touched them and withdrew her hand quickly. They felt nothing like her tail had. She tried to move them as she would have moved her tail but there were two of them.

"Oh, this is weird," she said, out loud.

The sound of her own voice startled her and she had no idea whether she was thrilled or panic-stricken.

"Think, Ruby," she told herself.

She lifted one foot and put it back and then the other foot and put it back. She wiggled her toes and could feel her confidence growing. She realised her bottom was most uncomfortable sitting on the rock. It wasn't at all like having a well-padded tail. With an impetuous lurch, she threw herself off the rock. She fell, flailing, into the water, shocked by how clumsy and ungainly she was now.

Ruby tried to kick but couldn't get her legs to work together. They seemed useless to her after her strong, powerful tail. She scooped and paddled with her hands while letting her legs kick pathetically. Somehow, she managed to reach the shore. Hauling herself onto the sand, she collapsed in exhaustion. That swim was the hardest, most graceless thing she had ever done.

While she caught her breath, she lay on her back where her gaze was drawn upwards by the noise of the mewing gulls.

"What are they up to today?" she thought, as she watched their erratic behaviour.

Above them, the sky was alive with the clouds racing across a patchwork of blue and grey. As she looked up, a shaft of sunlight broke free and she followed it with her eyes to where it bounced off the mirrored blue.

"The sea seems very lively today," she thought, propping herself up on her elbows to get a better look.

Shimmering aqua danced amongst the dark, broodingly dangerous whole. Ruby shivered with excitement. The gulls, the sky, the sea, all reflected her own agitated, nervous state of mind.

"I'm going to walk," she said to herself, and gave a high-pitched giggle.

Like all the mer, Ruby had spied on humans before, even though they weren't supposed to. Last year, she had done *Human Studies* at school so not having a tail made her believe that she'd be mistaken for a human quite easily. She stood and took her first shaky step on the sand. It wasn't nearly as easy as she had hoped. Mer babies swam as soon as they were born so it hadn't occurred to Ruby that it wouldn't be the same with humans and walking. Wobble, wobble, fall, went Ruby. Up she got and tried again. She was going to master this even if she had to try all day. Instinctively, she put her arms out to keep her balance. After an hour or so of concentrated hard work, Ruby was leaving a trail of happy footprints behind her on the beach.

The crunch of the sand between her toes delighted her. She squeezed them down into it and then let them stretch out. Toes were such funny things; like stubby fingers. The ground was pushing itself up against her feet. Little bits of shell jabbed her flesh and slippery seaweed had her waving her arms about and falling over afresh. There was a new world of sensation rising up through her feet.

She padded to the water's edge and stood where the sea washed over them. Each time the tide surged up and covered her feet, it then pulled back, sucking the sand from under and around them. It was tickly and so much fun. Laughing with joy, she called to the gulls overhead.

"Look at me."

She then realised there was a reason why the gulls were behaving so strangely. They were shrieking hysterically further along the beach. Curious, she went closer to see and to her horror, she saw a smack of jellyfish marooned on the beach. She raced towards them, flapping her arms.

"Get away! Shoo!" she shouted at the gulls, who retreated to a safe distance to scream their anger and waggle their heads in her direction.

"What are you doing here? Oh, I must help you," she said to the jellyfish.

Their bodies trembled and shuddered so she knew they were still alive. She glanced around, her mind buzzing as she scooped handfuls of water over the stranded jellyfish. There had to be a way of rescuing them without being stung. On the high tide line, she spied some razorbill shells.

"They'll do," she thought. "I can use them to push them back into the sea."

15

Running up, she grabbed a handful then started back on her mission. The first two shells broke under the weight of the jellyfish, so she put two together for extra strength and managed to get a few of the jellyfish away from danger. Wading into the sea, she drove them out against the incoming tide.

"Back! Back you go!" she cried, shoving the water with her hands.

At first, the jellyfish just lay there, stunned and heavy with sand, but as they got into deeper water, they started to swim. With their tentacles streaming behind them, they opened and closed their caps in a fluid motion. Ruby clapped her hands above her head while jumping up and down.

"Yes!" she shouted.

Her joy was cut short back on the shore; some of the beached jellyfish had died and one was unlikely to survive. Desperation drove her and she rolled it over the sand and into the surf, where it sat forlornly on the current. Even when she managed to get it further out, it didn't revive.

Engulfed by sadness at their death and her failure to save them all after such a big effort, she threw herself on the strand and sobbed great, gulping tears. The salt stung the cuts from the shells on her hands which she had been unaware of until then. Her sense of misery increased, Ruby dragged one hand across her nose and cried until her eyes were swollen, pink, and all dried out. As she sat there, the sky cleared and the sun came out. Ruby shut her eyes and turned her face to its kindly warmth. Her tummy rumbled loudly, startling her. She was on her own and would have to find something to eat.

She wandered down to the rocks, which were being revealed by the retreating tide, and snacked on some mussels, whelks, and winkles. Prising them apart with a razorbill shell she went "mmm" as she ate. Shellfish were a rare, yummy treat for the mer.

A rustling, rummaging noise made her jump up with a start. For a moment, everything had been forgotten as she was so absorbed in her eating. She felt very exposed standing right out in the middle of the bay; anyone could see her. She wasn't alone anymore. Who was it? She squinted at the scrubland at the top end of the beach and couldn't see anything but there was definitely something there. The landweed was swaying in and out. Her eyes rolled wildly about, searching for cover. Ruby dropped into a crouch, cloaked herself with her hair, and edged closer to the rocks. The sudden, unexpected fear left her dry-mouthed and sure that her heart's tumultuous beat was ringing round the bay.

Chapter 3

"Rrap, rrap, rrap," went a wild, demonic being as it raced away from the rustling landweed and headed off down the beach, chasing the gulls. Ruby breathed out slowly. It wasn't a human.

"Phew," she thought. "I don't want to meet anyone now, no way."

Even though she had legs, she realised she didn't feel human or know how to behave as if she was one. She just felt like herself. She shuffled forwards slightly to get a better view, but couldn't see very much and was frightened of leaving her hiding place. She could still hear the high-pitched, startling noise. All she had seen was a ball of brown fur flying inches above the sand. She cast her mind back to *Human Studies* and couldn't think of any animals that flew close to the ground except for birds. Birds soared in the sky. That was no bird! Thankfully, the racket was getting further away and then faded to nothing. Nonetheless, Ruby stayed crouched out of sight, too nervous to give up what little shelter she had. If anyone was there, she imagined that from a distance they would mistake her for a rock, curtained as she was by her long, red-brown hair. She hugged her arms around her knees to blend in more and smiled to herself, pleased with her plan.

Beginning to feel stiff and uncomfortable from staying in the same position so long, she was on the point of stretching out when the creature reappeared. Its tongue was hanging out and it was panting. Every few steps, it paused to have a good sniff and scratch at something in the shingle.

Ruby froze and prayed, "Don't let it find me. Please don't let it find me."

No longer airborne, it meandered along the beach on four legs, sometimes trotting, head held high, other times investigating with its nose rubbed into the sand. Its scruffy coat was rough brown with flecks of black in it. Only its ears seemed soft like dark sealskin and they moved up and down as if speaking. Ruby had never seen a creature like it in the sea. It had two intelligent, brown eyes with mischief sparkling within. They reminded Ruby of dolphin eyes. She squinted at the creature – was it smiling?

Suddenly it spotted Ruby. The loud yipping started up again which made Ruby jump and, in her panic, she sprang to her feet and set off as fast as she could. The creature came bounding after her, full of excitement, intent on the chase. Ruby pounded along the beach but didn't seem able to escape the creature so she turned and headed up the dunes, further from the sea. The sand was softer here and her feet sank deep into it with each step. She found herself going slower and slower, aware of her heart thudding in her chest and her legs aching.

"Go away," she gasped at it, but it didn't.

Instead, it danced around her, barking and baring its teeth. She staggered to the top of the dune as the sand crumbled beneath her feet and knew she couldn't go any further. She had barely walked before, let alone run up a beach. Exhausted, she bent over and placed her hands on her thighs. It was her turn to pant now.

"I don't think I can outrun you," she wheezed at it.

To her amazement, it didn't attack her but stopped racing about, sat down, and looked up at her. Bravely, she reached out her hand. The animal inched closer and she was rewarded with a lick. Its tongue was warm, wet, and reassuring. Ruby relaxed and smiled at it. The small, previously-fierce animal edged closer still and nestled in beside her. She ruffled its ears gently which it seemed to like as it leant its head into her before rolling over onto its back with its legs in the air.

Ruby thought that this was very funny and a little chuckle escaped her. She said, "Not so scary now, are you?"

The creature settled beside her, leaning its weight against her. She felt great to have tamed this wild animal and slightly relieved not to be alone. The animals in the ocean didn't cuddle and neither were they furry. A warm glow of comfort rushed over Ruby at this wonderful experience.

"I don't know what kind of animal you are," she told it, "but as you are playful like the dolphins, I'll call you Dolph."

From then on, every time she caressed him she called him Dolph so that he would get used to his new name. In return, Dolph stayed with her, greeting her with merry "rraps" and dances.

Now that she had a companion, Ruby thought that she should leave the sheltered bay behind and go inland to find humans. She patted her bag for reassurance. It gave a little squelch as she did so which reminded her of the catfish and dogfish hidden inside it. Down at the shoreline, she let them swim away. She still had her most treasured possession, her mirror, but looked around to see if there was a memento she could take from the bay. It couldn't be anything alive. Running along the high tide line was a dark, snaky border of debris. Rummaging through it, she found seaweed, shells, driftwood, and unappealing bits of discarded, broken stuff, obviously from humans. In the end, she wrapped a few more razorbill shells in seaweed and put them in her bag.

"Come on, we'd better find a way off this beach," she said.

Together they set off and Ruby headed to where she thought her friend had appeared. Walking up and down, she couldn't find anywhere that looked like a way out. She tried to get past the long sea-grass but the sharp blades cut her and the sea holly pricked her. Tears of frustration and pain stung her eyes.

"There must be a way without getting scratched by this nasty weed," she told Dolph. "How did you get here?"

She walked slowly along the edge of the scrub, fearful of going in again. So busy was she, searching for a way in, that she failed to notice the spiky thorns on the ground before they jabbed her foot.

"Oww!" she cried, clutching it to her while hopping on the other foot.

Landing heavily, she would have sunk into despair if Dolph had not rushed up to her with licks, warmth, and concern. She knelt down and hugged him tight.

"I can't get out of here. We're stuck. Oh, what will we do?" she asked him.

"Rrap," he replied, and bounded away from her, disappearing into the long grass ahead.

"Please don't leave me," Ruby entreated, and his little face poked out, framed by the grass, with an impatient look.

Ruby hurried over to where he was and discovered a concealed opening with a half-trodden path leading her onwards.

"You are clever. Is this the way? Did you come this way?" she asked.

The path led them safely between the rough grasses and over some dunes before it began to climb upwards. There was so much to see that Ruby's eyes never stopped moving from one thing to the next.

A small, yellow-brown bird perched on a twig, caught her eye. It cocked its head at her and went "twee, twee, twee, trrr, trrr."

"Oh, Dolph, have you ever seen anything so sweet?" she said.

She moved towards it and it flew up further off, singing its pretty song. She couldn't resist following it off the path where her feet sank into the boggy ground. When she lifted them up, they were covered in sticky mud. Thrilled, she stepped in a second time and did a little hop and then a big jump. The sludge squelched around her legs, making 'plock, plock' sounds as it did so. One of her legs got slightly stuck and she wobbled on it, shouting, "Waah, waah," with delight before yanking it free. She jumped right back in to feel that wonderful, stuck-pull sensation again. The bird continued its song, sitting on a branch close by.

"Come on, Dolph, join in!" Ruby called, but Dolph snuffled around until, bored, he lay on the path and yapped at her.

Laughing, Ruby threw herself on the ground beside him, stroking his silky ears. Fluidly, his body slumped against her until he was lying on his back with his tail sweeping the ground. His adoring, hazel eyes gazed up at her imploringly. Ruby scratched his tummy then rolled over and copied him, waving her arms and legs in the air, too. Flecks of mud fell on her face and she happily brushed them away.

Once they stopped playing, Ruby turned to look back the way they had come. The deserted bay had shrunk so that it seemed possible to scoop it up in her hand. She was astonished. For what had seemed days, not hours, the bay had been her first home on the land. In her mind, it felt like an enormous universe. Yet there was the whole of it on display, from one end to the other. She shook her head in disbelief. How could it become smaller like that? This world on the land was so confusing. Everything she knew and took for granted was scrambled. At least the sun, sea, and sky were still there, steady and true.

The sky was the clearest blue and the sea calm and smooth. The intensity of the day had passed and above the sea hung the sun, haloed with gentle pink, blue, and orange hues. Ruby was reluctant to leave the sea. She could feel the rhythm of the waves moving in time with her heart. Her body swayed to the beat and her sense of oneness with the ocean overwhelmed her. There and then she would have rushed back but her sharp elbows balanced on her knees reminded her afresh that she had no tail. She was a legged, land-bound creature now. Sadly, she bent her head into Dolph and rubbed her cheek against his fur.

With Dolph beside her, she clambered up the last stretch of the cliff and got her first sight of an expanse of land. What a surprise greeted her.

"A sun. Another sun!" she spluttered. "Are there two suns in the human world?"

Chapter 4

Open-mouthed, Ruby stared at the second sun. In her astonishment, she glanced over her shoulder at the first sun. It was a mistake. She put her hands up to her eyes and stepped backwards. The world spun while multi-coloured spots flickered about in her vision. She blinked but still they came; red, blue, and yellow lively dots growing, shrinking, and then dying away. She knew never to look directly at the sun but in her confusion forgot. Eric would have laughed at her foolishness.

When the colours finally settled, she turned back to the second sun and risked a cautious glimpse of it. Inch by inch, she found she could stare fully at it without it dazing her. Relieved, she saw that it was fainter than the first sun. Its glittering light shone between the brownish-grey stems of the land coral that broke the view into small, elongated pictures. Twinkling cheekily at her like the sun's reflection on a flat sea, Ruby wanted it, whatever it might be.

"What is it Dolph?" she asked, but Dolph was too busy snuffling nose down in the grass to bother to reply.

Screwing up her eyes thoughtfully as she peered at the sparkly thing, Ruby decided that it couldn't be very far away and that she would go and find it. Setting off with Dolph at her heels, she wound her way over soft tussocks of hairy grass and wind-flattened shrubs. The pale green landweed was quite different to the bruised-purple, rubbery seaweed she knew. Its fine, feathery fronds brushed against her legs as she walked and rippled in the fresh breeze coming from the sea. The going became harder as the path disappeared but Ruby and Dolph were beckoned on by the glinting beacon.

A swathe of clouds covered the sun for an instant, making the bright guide fade and dull then reappear just as vibrant. Stopped in her scramble by its disappearance, Ruby suddenly understood that it wasn't a sun but only an illusion of one. The land was so different from the ocean. Here the earth sucked the sunshine up, except for the shiny jewel. No wonder she wanted to find it. Her home was illuminated with dazzling echoes of brilliance cascading through the water.

Ruby smiled as she remembered playing one of her favourite games with Eric. They would wait for a day with a strong sun and plenty of white, scudding clouds and swim up until their heads popped out of the water. The sound of their laughter was sharper in this radiant world while below them, spirals of golden light circled away. Treading water, they watched for a good, sunlit shaft to catch and race downwards as far as they could. Guessing which one would be a winner was part of the fun. Eric would shout, "Go!" and they would propel themselves as hard and fast as possible to beat the approaching clouds before they found themselves back in the murk.

Eric preferred days when the water was as still as a polished mirror, throwing rays all around. Ruby didn't. Squinting in the brightness, she pulled her long hair in front of her eyes, mumbling complaints like mad. Eric's eyes were darker and he could bear it for longer which also meant that it was easier for him to guess where the tunnels would appear. He had a victory dance and would cry out, "Champion, champion!" until Ruby was infuriated.

Ruby preferred it when there were ripply waves so that she had a better chance of winning. Choppy or still, the game always ended in the same way. Ruby, getting fed up of losing, would forget about racing and dart off to play alone between the fluting channels in the deeper water. Eric would get annoyed with her and announce that she was the loser. They would have an all-out fight, swim in opposite directions, and not speak for the rest of the day. Why was she never allowed to win? It was so unfair. Not that they played anymore, now that Eric was above such childish games.

Mooching on, Ruby was glad that Eric wasn't here. This was her adventure and if he was here he would try to be the boss, as he always did, wanting it all his own way. Whatever path Ruby had been on was nowhere to be found. Instead, she waded through the undergrowth. In places, the foliage came up to her waist, slowing her down. There were curved stems with tiny thorns attached which scratched. She had learnt to be careful of them. Her cheeks were pink with the effort and she kept brushing insects away from her face. She missed not being able to rise up and above the plants as she did in the sea.

"How do humans manage life just on one level?" she wondered. "It makes it so much more difficult. If only I could float over all this."

Looking up, she spotted the little yellow bird fluttering along beside her and wished she could fly. While she was getting flustered and short-tempered, struggling against the wall of leaves, it continued to sing happily. Even though her legs ached with the walking she'd done, the shimmering object wasn't getting any closer. It was further than she had imagined. It didn't help that she kept losing sight of it by veering off course when she was deep in the green or down in a ditch.

After a while, she started following the way Dolph took. It meant crawling under some thick landweed but he seemed to find his way with a confidence she lacked. As she scrambled up a small hillock, she lost her footing and fell, twisting her ankle. Crossly, she bashed at the plants with her arms and sat heavily on a clump of bracken.

"I want to go home," she thought, feeling very fed up.

Rubbing her sore ankle, she looked about. With the sun dropping in the sky, the tall, slim stems of some of the land coral glowed softly silver. Nearby, a cluster of them stood out starkly against the darker shapes. Dolph was in front of her and heading purposefully towards them. Getting up, Ruby hobbled after him.

As she got nearer, she saw that there were five slender, pearly corals forming a circle around the most extraordinary plant she had ever seen. Its thick trunk was bent double, making an arched doorway. Gashes lined its length where it had been injured when it fell. They had created scars as it healed and by a miracle, it was still alive. Ruby ran her hands over the coarse bark and the lipped wounds that made her think of silenced mouths. She put her ear against them to hear its secret but the coral was quiet.

"Whatever caused this must have been very powerful," Ruby thought.

Sprouting from its top, which was now the same height as the base of the trunk, were tender, pliable branches with green, fingered leaves and petite, creamy-white petals with a sweet scent. Water bubbled near the edge of the clearing and then trickled away into the surrounding ground. Squatting down, Ruby splashed some on her face, letting it drip into her mouth. Bending lower, she slurped up a long and refreshing drink.

Feeling restored, she wiped her wet chin with the back of her hand as she took in her surroundings. Bell-shaped, purple-blue flowers nodded in the circle's shelter. Dolph made himself at home by having an energetic roll amongst them. The prize of the second sun forgotten, Ruby started to climb the trunk. The branches stepped up like a ladder and it was a simple thing to get to the top and sit there, swinging her legs.

"Hey," she shouted, delighted to be so high.

Gazing up, she felt the leaf-fringed sky pulling her higher while at the same time the earth dragged her back down and it made the world spin, leaving her dizzy. Clutching the tree, she shut her eyes for a moment until the world steadied. When she opened them, she was peering into the centre of the land coral. The inside was cool, dark, and hollow. From a few holes nearer its base, light filtered in, creating shadows which gave it a solemn air. Ruby crept forwards.

"Hello," she called into its heart, and her words were swallowed up.

Jumping down, Ruby landed and ran round the trunk spying, one-eyed, through the cracks. How was it still living with an empty middle and bent double? Ruby had never seen anything survive against the odds like that. Yet it was very much alive. She fervently wished that her Nan could see it. As a Healer, she would have been impressed.

"Dolph, come here."

Dolph ambled towards her and was surprised when she scooped him up into her arms. At first, he struggled awkwardly and scratched her by accident.

"Dolph, let's go under here three times and say 'friends forever'. Three is a lucky number, my Nan said so, and this is a lucky coral."

With this, he settled as she stroked his ears gently. Singing, "friends forever" loudly, Ruby skipped under and around the doorway.

Sinking to the ground and letting Dolph go, Ruby felt oddly happy. As she relaxed, she gave a little tremble and then a bigger one. Her teeth knocked together and began to go "brrrr". Once begun, they couldn't stop chattering and then her arms started shivering, and her chest. The skin on her arm was raised up with tiny bumps and standing to attention on each one was a hair. Her toes felt numb so she wriggled them. It was a peculiar sensation, as if they didn't belong to her. Reaching to touch them, she could feel how cold they were. She shuddered, hugging her knees to her while pulling her hair over her to make a blanket. Her face crumpled in confusion. She had never felt anything like it and had no word to explain it. Overwhelmed by self-pity and exhaustion, she crawled to the leaf-filled hollow under the arch. Lying down in a tightly-curled ball, she was asleep before she realised how tired she was.

Dolph carefully kicked leaves on top of her until she was almost completely hidden and then stretched out, back to back beside her. A breeze whispered through the trees above, sighing gently as it did so. The last scrap of evening left the day and night rolled in. A wobbly, gibbous moon adorned the sharp, clear sky bedecked with bright stars. As Ruby slept contentedly, a dark shadow flew overhead, blocking the moonlight. Dolph stirred, raising his head a little and shifting his body so that he was even closer to Ruby. The shadow merged into the encompassing blackness and was gone. Ruby and Dolph slept peacefully on, their slumber undisturbed.

Chapter 5

Early that same morning, just before light pricked the sky, the witch woke with a single tear trickling down her cheek. She sat up and smiled as her heart beat with joy. She knew this feeling. The last mer child was approaching. She had waited so long and so calmly. However, now that the moment was almost upon her, she felt so excited that her patience twirled out of her and away.

To try and relax, she put the kettle on to make herself her favourite noxious brew of chocolate treachery. As the boiling water was poured over the leaves, the aroma rose up in the steam. Inhaling deeply, the witch licked her lips slowly. It tasted deliciously of a betrayal to come.

Clutching the hot mug between her fingers, she stepped with a new lightness outside onto the dewy, morning grass. Digging her long-nailed toes into the soil, the power of the land flushed through her. Her skin itched with anticipation as freshness filled her, and she threw back her head and cackled loudly. The sound echoed through the trees, shivering their core with intangible fear and disturbing the birds in their sleep. Up, flew the birds, up and further up, filling the sky with a dark miasma of fluttering anxiety and noisy clamour.

As if called at the same time, the witch's companion arrived in the clearing beside her. He was as dark as the night with a quiff of golden feathers adorning his handsome head. Sharp, yellow eyes sat either side of it. He waddled towards her.

"Welcome, Goose," she said. "The mer child is on her way. We must make haste."

"Ahh-honk," came his answer, strong and loud.

The witch hitched up her long skirt as she mounted Goose.

"Ahh-honk," he repeated, slow and deep, as she settled onto his back.

With her shadowy hood pulled low over her head, they rose up into the sky like an ominous black cloud. Only her pale, purple-veined legs were visible; creamy twin moons gliding through the darkness into the dawn.

All day they journeyed until they came to the cottage by the sea. The witch paced round and round, muttering silent, breathless spells as she did so. She willed the mer child onwards. The trees and land obeyed her and closed around Ruby, locking the road behind her and blocking her way back to the sea's embrace. Her blood pulsed in time with the rhythm of Ruby's pace, drawing her ever in. Her happiness overflowed as she stretched and grew with it. She became younger and taller-looking than the day before as years of waiting fell from her. She rubbed her hands together with glee.

Suddenly, a jolt shot through her. The mer child had stepped off the time-worn path to her door. She furrowed her brow with concentration, trying to sense where the child had gone. Nothing. This had never happened in the past. The other mer children had all arrived in the beautiful, frightening

33

stygian hours. Drat and double drat. She knew she could not search for her until night came when it was possible to ride Goose under cover of an inky sky. Vexation rippled up and down her limbs and crossed her face, making her as ugly as an old man's thick, yellowed toenails. She raised a foot to stamp it on the ground hard but held it there, poised. She had no choice but to hold in her wrath. Unleashing it now could warn the mer child of danger. Where could she be?

Out in her garden, she called the gulls to her. Perching on the roof of her cottage, they wagged their heads in her direction.

"Where is the mer child?" she demanded of them.

They mewed news of the child's arrival but were quickly distracted by sulky complaints about how she had ruined their fun with the jellyfish.

"Stop your whingeing," she snapped.

"We saw her leave, we saw her leave, she is coming, we watched just like we should," they flapped and pleaded.

With a curt wave of her hand, the witch dismissed them. As one, they lifted into the sky and flew away, relief beating from their wings. Deep in thought, the witch moved through the garden. This was not as it should be and she would have to be extra cunning with this one. Were there still pockets of trees with older magic than hers that might dare to oppose her? If so, she would find them and burn them to the ground. Pacing up and down like a trapped prisoner, she waited for daylight to fade to nothing so that she could go and look for the child.

As dusk descended, her soft squawk brought Goose at double quick time. Even Goose trembled when she whispered, as it was more fearful than when she stormed around in a temper. Together they flew backwards and forwards across the land and to the edge of the sea looking for, but not finding, any trace of the mer child.

Ill at ease, immeasurably cross, and exhausted, the witch returned to the cottage as day was breaking. Goose hobbled off for a rest while the witch crashed pots about in the kitchen. Eventually, she threw herself down in her floral armchair and shut her eyes. For a moment, there was silence and then it was broken as her snores ricocheted around the cottage.

The sun was streaming through the window, filling the house with warmth, when she woke. Humphing, she grabbed a basket and decided to soothe her rattled mind by going for a walk to collect mushrooms. Mushroom soup was always good for clearing her thinking. At all costs, she must remain calm. Once outside, with nostrils flaring, she sniffed the air.

"All is not lost," she muttered to herself.

Chapter 6

When Ruby first woke, only specks of starlight danced in the blackness above her and she shut her eyes and slept on. This time, she did not fall as deeply and a series of images played themselves out. A warm sense of being safe and happy stole into her slumber. Nan was with her and together they were helping an injured seal. It was so vivid that she heard Nan's firm but gentle voice offering reassurance. Gradually, reluctantly, she came to, shaking off the dream world, struggling to believe in all yesterday's adventures. Surprise and shock overtook her as she came face to face with reality. There were her legs, still real. Touching her feet, they remained numb with cold, as if they belonged to someone else. She drew them towards her, tucking them close while rubbing them hard to get some sensation back. The iciness of them seeped into the rest of her, the chill leaving her miserable and lonely.

Thoughts of her mum preparing food floated, unbidden, into her mind and she felt a pang of homesickness mixed with hunger. What would they be doing? Would they be looking for her?

She imagined them all at home. Before school yesterday, Mum had given her a rare turtle's egg for breakfast as a treat. It had been soft and runny. Eric had left early so it was just the two of them. As Mum passed by, she had stroked Ruby's hair lovingly but then Erin's Mum had called. Mum had talked too fast and laughed too loudly to their neighbour and afterwards she had fallen into a faraway, preoccupied state.

Since Nan had gone, Mum chatted too brightly, her laugh seemed false, and sometimes she stared into space, lost. Until now, she hadn't thought about how her mum felt because, more than anything, she had wanted Nan to come back. Without Nan, they didn't fit together as a family. Being here on the land was the first time her sadness at the loss of Nan had lifted. It was difficult to brood when life was all new, both thrilling and scary.

Dad was worse. He had bumped into her yesterday morning. Ruby remembered that he had been muttering away to himself. All he had said was, "Oh, you?" in a distracted manner before going on his way.

"I'm Ruby," she had said to his departing back, but he hadn't turned round.

Lately, he had been away working and she hadn't seen him very often. He had an important job but she wasn't really sure what he did. She smiled at the memory of how, when she'd been little, she thought he played flipball every day. Probably, he would be out looking for her. She hoped so.

Eric would be acting cool with his friends at school. He would be the last to notice what she did or where she went. They might not have missed her quite yet. There were many days when she came home late, as she liked to go exploring and would forget the time. It felt strange to realise how wrapped up in themselves all her family were but she was really, truly alone now, except for Dolph.

Her only comfort was his warm back beside her. She rolled over towards him and put out a hand to stroke his ears. Her reward was a wet lick across the face.

"Urgh," she said, wiping her face with her hand, while laughing and stroking his ears.

The morning sun was risen, sending dappled rays through the overhead branches. Sitting up, Ruby rubbed her eyes and scratched her head before pulling bits of leaves out of her hair. Loving thoughts of Nan lingered, lying snugly over her and she reached for the bag with the treasured mirror in it. It wasn't there. It had gone. Somehow, the bag must have come off in the night. Flustered, she groped frantically about in her leaf-bed until she found its familiar shape. To her relief, when she checked inside, the mirror was still there. Her fingers closed tightly around the handle. Immediately, she felt better.

Shutting her eyes, she whispered, "Nan, what should I do?"

At that exact moment, the thought crept into her mind that the mirror might not be safe with her. She clutched it to her, taken aback by the notion. It had been Nan's and she valued it above everything else. It was her secret and she had kept it hidden with her. Nobody knew about it, nobody. Not even her mum or Eric, and how much had she wanted to tell them and say, "Look what Nan gave me."

But she hadn't. A little smug smile played over her face as she remembered the day Nan had given it to her. The two of them had gone off wandering together and meandered further than usual. How tight-lipped her mum became over their trips!

She said to Ruby, "I despair of you, Ruby. You will end up just like your Nan."

Although this was meant to give Ruby pause, she had been delighted. Who better to be like than her amazing Nan? Nan was one of the last Healers and was discreetly sharing some of her knowledge with Ruby. Mum would be furious if she knew. She didn't want her to 'go down that current', as she put it.

When she had been young, her mother had chosen not to be a Healer and disapproved of Healers and their 'nonsense'. Nan told Ruby that she was a natural and Ruby had glowed, inside and out, with pride.

Once, far away from the colony, they had swum low into a cave and Nan had shown her some lichen growing on its edges. Quite unexpectedly, she had stopped and taken both of Ruby's hands, sandwiching them between her own. She looked, unblinking, into Ruby's eyes with a new intensity, before saying, "Ruby, I have something that I want you to look after for me."

She had wrapped Ruby's hands around the mirror, and then clasped them together, holding her gaze.

"This is our heirloom. My mother gave it to me. The handle is very rare as it is made from narwhal horn. The narwhals gave it to us as a gift of thanks. You mustn't let anyone know that you have it and must NEVER, NEVER let anyone else see it, not your mum, or your dad, or Eric. This is very important, Ruby. Can you do this?"

As she spoke, tears had coursed down Nan's cheeks. A mixture of feelings churned around Ruby; joy at being of enough value to be trusted and distress because Nan didn't cry, but she had nodded.

"Good, I believe you," Nan smiled, with relief.

It wasn't long after this that Nan had disappeared. Whenever she was alone, Ruby would slide her fingers into her bag and touch the mirror for succour. She didn't know why it was special and felt stupid for not having questioned Nan more about it when she had had the chance.

They had searched for Nan everywhere but no one had even heard a whisper of her. It had been a while now and everyone said she was gone for good. They had a knowing, 'grown-up' priggishness about them when they said it. This made Ruby really, really cross and she refused to believe it. Part of her was always looking, expecting Nan to appear out of the seaweed, or from a dark cave, with her warm smile.

The mirror was her only treasure yet the inexplicable urge to hide it was becoming very powerful and overwhelming. Shivering at the thought of it being lost or taken from her, she hunted around for a hiding place. The curious land coral? Of course, that was the answer! After sheltering her all night, now it could shelter the mirror. She was sure to find her way back to it again, as it was so unusual. The frown that had been creasing her forehead lifted as she smiled, happy to have worked out a solution.

On the ground, she found a large leaf and wrapped the mirror carefully in it, securing it with a strand of long grass, before looking for a safe nook. At first, she thought of stuffing it deep into the bed where she had slept but Dolph put paid to that idea by digging a hole there straight away.

"Thanks," she said to him. "I take it that's not such a great plan?"

Dolph, as if in answer to her question, leapt against the trunk of the tree, barking.

"Oh, inside the land coral," said Ruby. "Why didn't I think about that?"

Climbing up the tree again, she peered into its empty heart for a niche. Leaning precariously into its mysterious depths, she spotted a sort of shelf-pocket. Reaching as far as her arm could stretch, she tucked the mirror in securely. Scrambling back, she squinted down into the gloom and could only just see where it was, but thought no one else would. Anyway, who would come here and why? Satisfied that it was well hidden, she climbed down. Picking up her bag, she gave the tree a pat before walking away from her night-time shelter.

The land stretched in front of her, full of the awakening day's expectation. Ruby stood on her tiptoes, gazing excitedly out at it. Slowly, she sank down onto her heels. It all seemed the same – an unbroken view of large and small land corals. Where were the houses, the humans? She both wanted and was afraid to meet a human, but she needed to, now that she was one. Otherwise, how would she live?

Once, her *Human Studies* teacher had organised a special excursion to see human dwellings at night. Her dad and some other parents had come along as helpers. All the grown-ups had acted nervously and Ruby had sensed their fear. She and her friends had been anticipating the trip for ages and were jumpy. Poor Erin and two other girls had got the giggles so badly that they weren't allowed to come and were taken home, missing out on the adventure.

Under the cover of night's obscurity, they had swum dangerously close to the shore, as near as they could get while staying safe.

41

They had seen some yellow lights glowing from a row of shapes.

"Look closely," their teacher had said. "They call those 'houses' and go in and out of them. They disappear inside them and the yellow light appears when it's dark. Look at the straight edges and you will see that it is not natural. The line does not flow at all."

The mer children were truly astonished. In the sea, everything flowed.

Ruby remembered asking, "Why do they want to do that?" and wrinkling her nose at the grown-ups' answer.

She knew then that the grown-ups didn't know. Her teacher had said that humans built houses because they were afraid of the world outside and liked to hide away from it. Ruby wondered how anyone could live without fluid lines around them and how you made them different.

Later, she had tried to get some stones into a neat pile but they refused to obey. They balanced in a higgledy-piggledy way and soon toppled over. The mer were at ease in their surroundings and the thought of living with boundaries was really odd. There had been a clamour of questions about it back at school, as the class had struggled to understand. Afterwards, the eerie visit and strangeness had stayed with them.

"Duh," she mock-slapped her head. "The shiny thing must be a house."

Yesterday, it had jumped out at her but with her jumbled feelings today, she had forgotten about it. First, the mirror, and then thoughts of humans, had got in the way. Going there had felt so right. It had been vibrant and alive. Ruby scanned the land for it but couldn't see it.

"Where has it gone and where have I come from?" she wondered.

In the ocean, she was really good at finding her way but here everything was so flat, making it impossible to tell one place from another. How could it have disappeared? Was that a flash in the distance? She scrunched up her eyes as she was facing the sun but that must be it, she decided.

A little skip of hope entered Ruby's step as she set off.

Chapter 7

In spite of her new eagerness, Ruby found herself casting glances behind her. Without the mirror, she felt weightless and gave lingering looks to the arched tree until it was out of sight. Just as it disappeared from view, Dolph echoed her feelings by turning and barking in its direction.

Ruby sighed and patted him, saying, "Come on."

The constant ache that missed her mum and family lifted as her fascination with the shiny jewel became stronger. Like the buildings her teacher had shown her, it grew out of the ground with a symmetry she hadn't seen in the ocean. Its sides made perfect straight lines while the trees swayed and bent in the breeze, their branches sharply elbowed and at every angle imaginable. Her glimpse of the night-black dwellings hadn't prepared her for how beautiful it would be. The walls were decorated with oyster and mussel shells and appeared to wink at her as their pearlescent insides caught the morning sun. Ruby peered closer. She could have sworn that from under its seaweed-fringed roof, it was giving her a welcoming smile. Captivated, she smiled back.

Encouraged, she and Dolph circled slowly around it, hugging a low, stone wall bordering its garden. In time, they found themselves face to face with a magnificent whale's jawbone, standing proudly over a gate. Ruby gaped at it, feeling cowed by its height and size. She placed a hand on her heart in shock that it had once been a whale. Whales were her friends and it seemed to be at odds with the happy house to have the destruction of such an amazing animal marking the threshold. Even to Ruby, it was obviously an entrance; a both challenging and inviting one. She paused, confused and uncertain what to do. Glancing anxiously around, she tip-toed closer to the gate and gave it a gentle push. It clattered open loudly, startling her into letting it go, then rattled shut. Jumping back, she hunkered down as small as she could make herself, ready to bolt or hide. Wide-eyed, she looked at the house.

"What … ?"

The noise made Dolph wild and he began barking while racing madly backwards and forwards at the gate. After a time, he settled and silence fell over the house.

Ruby uncurled herself and asked hesitantly, "Is anyone there?"

Nobody came or answered her. It all remained as quiet as it had been minutes earlier. Ruby was at a loss what to do next. She had come too far to go back but how could she go ahead? Staying still, she squatted there for ages, feeling as if something was about to happen. Getting bored, Dolph, to her surprise, pushed the gate open with his nose and slipped through. In a panic that she might be left alone, she leapt up and followed him.

"Wait for me."

The gate banged behind her.

Once on the other side of the gate, she forgot her uncertainty of the moment before. For the first time on land, she felt as if she belonged. She had arrived in the place she was meant to be.

It was an oasis of calm, a lost mer child's boon. The air was refreshing and undisturbed by the slightest breeze. Even the heat from the sun barely settled on her skin while the path under her feet was cool. Looking down, she saw the purest white cockle shells inlaid into it. Bending to touch their familiar heart shapes, her hand brushed a plant that spilt over its edges. Its red stems contrasted oddly against the paleness of the path. A rich, heavy aroma wafted up to her so powerfully that Ruby felt as if she could taste it. It was like nothing she had ever smelt before; almost sickly sweet. She knelt down to savour it by rubbing her fingers between the deep, purple-black flowers.

"Mmm," she went, "it's so good."

Dolph seemed happy, too. Tail held high, he was off investigating, scampering amongst the flowerbeds to either side of the path, stopping to scratch and whine every so often. He was half hidden by a sea of vivid green and blue flowers, quite different from the dark, delicious-scented ones.

Ruby would have stood there longer but the path led straight up to a rough, wooden door. Drawn onwards, she turned towards it. Seeing her move, Dolph rushed to her side. In the middle of the door was a knocker in the shape of a conch shell. Ruby tentatively reached out a hand to touch it. As she did, the door swung open, encouraging her and Dolph in.

"Wow!" she said to him. "It likes us."

She felt a quiver of anticipation as she entered the cottage. Other people's places and belongings had always incited Ruby's curiosity. When she was younger and all the children had played happily together, the thing she wanted most was to be asked to play with a friend. Her mum would arrange it as a treat if she had been good. How she had loved to imagine what it would be like if she belonged to another family. She could have sisters instead of a brother, and new parents. It gave her a slightly spooky shiver just imagining it; she could be someone else in another home with a different life altogether. Of course, years had passed since a friend had invited her to play at their house.

The other mer girls had stopped 'playing' – they 'hung out' now. It all seemed to be secrets and whispering them to each other. Ruby wasn't popular enough to belong and ended up nervous and sure that they were putting her down. Boys, and who liked who, were what they gossiped about most. Well, Ruby didn't see why that was interesting! She had an annoying brother so where was the excitement in that? Not that the girls talked to the boys, anyway. When she did, they only saw it as a sign that she wasn't to be trusted.

She was different now. What would they think if they could see her here? They wouldn't believe that she, Ruby, had found this incredible place; that she had been chosen and was special.

Inside, with Dolph beside her, the humidity hit her. The closest sensation to it she had experienced was swimming from one water current into the next but this was so much more. Taken by surprise, she took a step backwards and would have fallen if the door hadn't been shut behind her. She stood there until the heat seeped into her cold fingers and toes, stinging them. Dancing in a small circle, she cried, "Ow, ow, ow," as she did so.

47

In time, the pain eased. Relieved, she peered out from under her hair to have a good look around. At first, everything blurred together. There was so much for her to see that she couldn't tell where one thing began and another ended. Slowly, the colours and fabrics, the various bits and pieces of 'stuff', materialised into individual objects, and Ruby was charmed by them all.

Dolph wasn't nearly as nosy and sniffed briefly around the room before settling himself in front of the stove. Seeing him so relaxed and at ease gave Ruby courage. She stepped off the mat at the door and into the room. The first things that drew her to them were some driftwood and large shells. Fortunately, they were straight in front of her and she couldn't resist picking them up, one by one, and turning them over as if they were old friends from the sea. So absorbed did Ruby become that she sat down on the smooth, stone floor with them.

There was an ammonite fossil. Ruby was stunned to find it here. Her teacher had shown them an ancient one from his collection which he had found in shallow water but it was small with the muted tones of a seal skin. He had been really proud of it. This fossil was exquisite. She traced her finger around its whorls. It was bigger than her hand and set in a chunk of honey-orange rock.

Next, she carefully handled a perfect, delicate sea urchin shell. The white was sprinkled with salmon pink flecks. She licked her lips as she savoured the memory of the delicious butter inside. Bringing it close, she tried to breathe in its flavour but such a long time had passed since the flesh had lived in it that there was no smell left. Very gently, so as not to break it, she placed it on the floor beside the ammonite.

In some ways, the driftwood was the most curious of all the pieces. It wasn't a plain, ordinary bit. Carved into it were intricate, deftly-cut figures of mer and humans set amongst waves and land corals. The wood had a simple, natural beauty of its own but the figures on it transformed it into something unique. Ruby spent a lot of time trying to work out the story chiselled on the driftwood and finally gave up.

A sharks tooth necklace seemed dull in comparison so she put it down quickly before picking up some coral. It had three round, frilled plates leaning against each other to form a bigger circle. It was an iridescent blue that was only found in the idyllic southern seas. She had never been there but tales of the seven seas were legendary to all the mer. Ruby had had *Sea Studies* at school for as long as she could remember. Rolling it from hand to hand, she stared into its oceanic depths, lost in a dream of home.

Eventually, she snapped out of her reverie to put on the sharks tooth necklace and dance about the room. As she felt the teeth, she realised that this was also special. The teeth were the smallest, sharpest, most even ones she had ever seen. These curios were the wealth and generosity of all the seas. Only someone who knew and understood the ocean could have gathered such an extraordinary collection of treasure.

"This is a safe and good place to be," thought Ruby, happily.

Spinning round in her dance, the other objects in the room started to become real. None of it was familiar to her but altogether it painted a picture that appealed to her.

There was a sofa which was covered in images of starfish and sea horses. Running her hands along the length of it, she put her cheek against its back. The tiny ends of the fabric tickled her face and left patterns of light and dark where she had rubbed it. Throwing herself down, she felt embraced by it and rolled into it, clutching a cushion to her chest. Dolph came over and climbed up beside her, licking her face.

"Dolph, stop it!" she shouted, falling off the sofa and onto the floor, leaving a trail of cushions behind her.

After that, she couldn't resist touching it all, discovering every single new thing. She imagined what it would be like if this was her house and she lived here all the time. The thought was so funny that bubbly, slightly hysterical giggles rose up. Soon, tears ran down her face and she no longer knew whether she was happy or sad. Ruby hiccupped loudly before delving into the delights of the room again.

She stopped at a knob on a dresser which fitted nicely in her hand. First, she tried twisting it. Nothing happened so she gave it a push. Again, nothing, so she pulled it quite hard and the drawer flew open. Quickly letting go, Ruby jumped away in surprise. The drawer tottered on the edge for a while and then stilled. Breathing out slowly, Ruby inched her way back to the drawer. Carefully, she jiggled it until it almost closed.

As it was shutting, her eyes were drawn to a knitted object lying on the top. She picked it up and turned it over. It had orange and red stripes. Either side were two gaps, big enough for her fingers to waggle through. Twirling it in her hands, she impulsively pulled it onto her head where it sat cosily. Keeping it there, she continued poking about.

Opening cupboards and peering inside at jars and packets and plates and pots and pans, she was amazed at the variety and texture of it all.

"Where are all the humans who live here and need all this?" she thought. "A huge colony must live here."

Dolph had settled himself in front of the glowing embers of the stove and gone to sleep, curled up in a ball. She gave him a loving gaze before turning away to climb the stairs. Reaching the top, she went through the first door she came to.

Upstairs was less chaotic. The first room she entered wasn't as big and there were fewer furnishings so it was easier on the eye. She walked slowly round, taking it all in. On one wall were some pictures. Pressing her nose up close, she spent ages inspecting them thoroughly. They were of humans, dressed in faded, mismatched outfits. They were young like her, with flowing hair and uncertain smiles but with an edge of pride showing in the way they held their shoulders. Ruby understood. She patted her new hat in a satisfactory way and nodded her approval.

"I seem human now," she mused, "but I still need to be more like them."

Some of the tales Nan had told her surfaced in her mind. They had been tales of mermaids who became human but they had never seemed real to her. After all, who spoke about 'mermaids'? It was just a quaint, old-fashioned word from an unreal time, long, long ago. They were only stories meant for little children. However, the mermaid had always ended up dressed in human garments and usually married a Prince, who appeared to be a fantastic boy.

No wonder she had thought it a fantasy – boys weren't like that!

Struggling to remember what the teacher had taught them in class, the lesson came back to her. She couldn't believe that this part of *Human Studies* had escaped her so far. They did cover themselves! It was another of those strange, human facts that they had all found odd. When the teacher had explained how humans wore clothes, all the girls had sniggered together. How could they be streamlined? Did they not get in the way and flap around? Why? They had rolled their eyes at each other and Ruby had laughed so much she had got into trouble but for that moment, she had belonged.

The memory made her feel warm inside. She was beginning to understand a little of why clothes were essential. There was no need to be slick and quick like a fish when you couldn't go up and down but were stuck on the ground all the time. Coming past the thorns yesterday, Ruby had wished for armour as strong as a crab's! And the wind whipped through you and around you, leaving your teeth knocking against each other and your skin exposed and vulnerable, like a peeled shrimp.

Clothes made sense. Feeling cheered and buoyed up, she started to snoop. There was a cupboard with drawers in; this time, she pulled on the handles carefully. All the clothes in it were squashy. She removed the first garment she found. Scrunched in her hand, it barely took up any space but when she let it go, two long tails fell away from the main body of it where there was a hole.

She carried it to the pictures for inspiration on how to wear it. There was none. Putting her hand in the opening, the fabric stretched so that she could see through it. Her skin could pass for wet sand.

"Humans are very strange," she thought.

Pushing her hand further down a pliable tube, she was startled by a loud 'rrrrip' sound. There was a hole with an ever-increasing ladder running away from it. Quickly, she withdrew her hand and stuffed them back in the drawer. She shut it with a guilty slam and opened another.

From this one, she pulled out a much sturdier garment. It stretched the length of her body and was wider than she was. Holding it up, she saw that the bottom end made a floppy tunnel while at the top there was a narrower opening with two thin flaps, like empty eels dangling at the sides. Ruby crawled into it until her head poked through. When she stood up, her arms were trapped so she twisted and turned until they were encased in the material. The colour was a deep blue and decorated with yellow moons and stars. It made her feel much better being covered up although it wasn't perfect, even slightly awkward. She had to keep holding her arms in the air to free her hands while lifting it up where it trailed on the ground. She tripped, stepping on the hem a few times before getting the hang of it.

"At least I am more human now," she decided, with a small, anxious smile.

On the other side of the room was a sash window set in the eaves. Crossing the room, she peered out of it. Being able to view the world from up above was a surprise. Sadly, as far as her eye could see, there weren't any other houses. There was the gate with the whale jawbone above it and the path. Looking down at the garden, she saw that the flowers were in beds the shape of mer people. She had been too close when she was on the ground to notice but it was very clear from up here.

"Wow!" she said. "That's amazing".

There were seven beds. One was empty while the other six were full of beautiful flowers, but the most incredible thing was that they had different flowers for the bodies and tails and faces. Each bed resembled an individual mer person. That one was a boy, and over there was a small girl. The flowers rippled in the breeze and the mer flower people quivered.

"Look at them. They are so real they could be alive," said Ruby.

Turning to rush outside and inspect them more closely, a movement in the trees caught her eye. The mer flower people forgotten, Ruby stared, big-eyed. Materialising from the woods was a person, a real person, coming here!

Chapter 8

Thwacking the trees and shrubs to the left and right, the witch made her way to the centre of the woods. As she approached, the songbirds stifled their trilling and fluttered away from her in fear. One small bird was too late and caught the sharp edge of her hand as she passed. The blow sent it somersaulting into the undergrowth of curly-fingered ferns to lie as if dead, too frightened to move. Deep in the stillest part of the wood where ancient earth magic lived, the witch stopped. From a tree, she pulled her cape of moss and draped it over her shoulders. She wrapped it tightly around her, feeling the potency of the land enter her being. Making herself comfortable on a tree stump, she waited until Goose flew through the trees to join her.

"Rrruk," he said, settling down.

Things were not as they should be, she ruminated, but she would triumph, even though the pattern had been broken. For the first time, one of the mer children had not arrived at her door in the menacing midnight hours but in the dawn of a new morning. The witch knew that her talents were born out of a primal blackness that she had moulded to serve her own ends. She was the only witch of land and sea and she was destined to win.

Casting her mind back, she savoured her last, unexpected meeting with a mer who had sprouted legs. The memory was so good that she guffawed abruptly like a pig, a loud and ugly snort. The trees drew away from her while the woodlice and centipedes scurried to hide under leaves and fallen bark.

She let her mind sink into the past. A woman, a grown woman, had arrived at her cottage. Her long hair and her dress fashioned from woven seaweed announced that she was mer while the lines on her face clearly showed her age. The witch had been snoozing in her chair when the gate had rattled open. Leaping up in alarm, she had the presence of mind to sneak a glance out of the window and spy on who had disturbed her. No one had taken her by surprise before and she did not like it. The gulls should have warned her, she decided with gritted teeth, but she would deal with them later. It was irritating and she wanted to shout rudely but then she furrowed her brow. Why had someone come to her hearth? There was nothing to do but find out. Adjusting her features to appear kindly, she opened the door a fraction and peeked around it as the woman was about to knock.

"Yes?" she asked, nicely.

"I have left my home in search of you."

The woman in front of her was not afraid. She stood up straight and did not avert her eyes, keeping them locked on the witch's own. The witch was discombobulated. Curiosity jabbed at her. Raising one eyebrow, she stared back at the woman.

"Come in," she rasped, as she fully opened the door.

The woman stepped over the threshold and with her came the powerful aroma of the sea. The deepest depths of the ocean seemed to swim into the cottage.

"Have some tea."

The witch poured a rich-coloured, well-brewed mixture into two cups and took the seat at the head of her table. She gestured to another seat. The woman paused, seeming to weigh up the offer for a moment, then took a place at the table. Streaks of grey lined her hair. She was older than the witch had first imagined. Sitting, the woman gazed into the teacup thoughtfully before raising her head to catch the witch's eye.

"I know what you are doing."

"I am having tea," the witch replied, craftily.

She took a sip of her tea then replaced the cup in the saucer with precision. She was in no hurry.

"I know you have the brush."

The woman was composed and collected.

"What brush?" The witch jerked her head to the side and widened her eyes in surprise.

This talk had taken an unexpected turn.

"The one that was stolen from my family, many years ago."

"What makes you think that you can come into my home and accuse me of stealing? You are my guest."

Caught off guard, the witch let self-righteous outrage fill her.

"I have come to ask for it back. I know that it is here," the woman replied, stubbornly.

The witch's mouth mumbled away as she chewed it over, "This woman is crazy. Who does she think she is, coming here and accusing me of theft! The brush is mine. It called to me so I took it. I lost my home and was cast out by the mer for the brush. If that isn't payment enough, I don't know what is!"

Her lip curled upwards in contempt as she stood up abruptly, knocking over the cups as she did so. The woman's tea spilt, running off the edge of the table and onto her lap. Steam rose from the seaweed dress. The woman stayed still as the witch towered above her.

"If you keep it, it will cause you harm in the end." Unruffled by the accident, the woman spoke with a quiet determination.

"What do you know of harm? I only have what is mine. You have come here to steal from me, I can tell. But you won't."

Riled by the woman's steadiness, the witch lost control of her temper, the pitch of her voice increasing.

The woman remained calm and insistent, even in front of the growing wrath. The witch's eyes became small and pinched, burning with fury as she spat out,

"A Healer. A great Healer are you? Coming here to ask me for help. How dare you!" Her eyes reduced further to venomous, narrow slits as she continued.

"You dare to come to me. Why? What has made you come here to my door? Are you in trouble, so much trouble that you have to come to me. Answer me." A note of triumphant cunning had entered the witch's voice.

The woman looked down at her hands and then up, to hold the witch's scrutiny without turning aside.

"The mer colony blames the theft on the Healers. The people say it was the Healers' fault for adopting you. Nothing had ever been stolen before. Nobody trusts each other now, least of all the Healers. We practice in secret, living separate lives. The mer need us. This grief will find its way to your door if you do not set things right and return the brush."

Smiling her warmest, oiliest smile while leaning close in, the witch asked, "And the mirror? Do you still have it? Where is it?"

"No, I don't have it." The woman's evenness was grating on the witch.

She snapped, "Have you hidden it? One good turn deserves another. I have invited you into my house and offered you tea. Now you tell me how to find it."

"I don't have it." She paused, adding too quickly, "And I don't know where it is right now."

Instantly, the witch could sense her weakness.

"Liar. You are a liar. Bring me the mirror and I will give you the brush."

"Rumours, there are rumours..." For the first time, the woman's quiet poise was shaken.

Standing tall, the witch pointed to the door and in tones of indignation, said, "There are *no* rumours about me. Return to wherever you came from and be an outcast amongst your kind. Do not come back here. You will not be welcome."

The woman got to her feet and made her way from the cottage, the clattering of the gate signalling her departure.

For a moment, the witch stayed in the same place, completely still. There was something familiar about the face. It reminded her of long ago and the Healer who had cared for her.

"Thinks she can get around me with pity," she thought. "The mirror still exists. That woman knew of it. I can feel it getting closer. Then ... then I will rule the seven seas and the land. Nobody will be able to stop me. I will have what I want!"

She screamed, "Goose! Make haste, for we will make sure she does not return to the sea and take her rumours with her."

"Wink, wink, wink," replied Goose, excitedly.

Flying over the land, they swiftly overtook the woman. She had walked further than the witch had anticipated, almost to the woods. Her head was down, deep in thought, as she strode out, and the soft sigh of Goose's wings on the wind did not make her turn. Seizing her advantage, the witch and Goose flew high, then glided, low and silent, right up behind her. The attack was sudden and well-planned. A single, mighty strike from the witch's stick and the woman collapsed onto her knees. Pounding her with the stick again and again, the woman finally keeled over until she lay, unmoving, on the ground. She had cried out with the first blow and then not made a sound.

With a squawk of satisfaction, the witch returned to her cottage. There would be no more rumours of her plans amongst the mer. Who would challenge her, now that this Healer had gone?

Dreams of the woman and the mirror brought her back to the present. Standing and shaking her moss cloak to the ground, she admired the bounty she had created. Covering her body were mushrooms of all shapes and sizes. Carefully, she ripped them from her skin, one by one. Each stung a little, just like tearing off a plaster. The pain was sweet and delicious. Tenderly, she placed them in her basket.

Emerging from the wood, there was a lightness in the witch's step as she sashayed towards the house. The hem of her dress swished damply against the dewy grass and she felt at one with the world, in spite of the sunny morning. The anxiety of the night before had faded and her confidence had returned.

Then Goose brought the news that the mer child had arrived and was in her lovely cottage, her mer child trap. It had worked again, enticing them in and enveloping them in its comforting embrace. Winding her hair into a neat bun, she rearranged her face into a kind, gentle expression, disguising all her jubilation under a false mask. She contented herself with letting her laughter rattle about inside her chest where it could not be seen. Only her right hand gave her away. Her high hopes would fly out of the ends of her fingers, making her flex them taut for a fraction of a second, then release them. It was the only sign of her true state of mind and she hid it behind her back.

Goose mirrored her feelings as he often did. He kept the same steady, unhurried pace, only occasionally allowing his neck to rise up stiff before letting it loosen and waddling on. After he had seen the mer girl on her way to the cottage, he had made haste to the witch's side. Together, they came in perfect harmony of purpose.

When the witch spotted Ruby, a shadow of a smile twitched at the corners of her mouth. Why, the child was jumping about with glee. It couldn't be more wonderful. Capturing this mer child was going to be simple. Six were bedded and biddable already. Some were easier than others. The white-haired mer boy, what was his name, had caused her no end of trouble but she was wiser now and those problems wouldn't happen again. She shifted her basket of mushrooms on her arm and looked at them lovingly. It had been a good morning's pickings.

Chapter 9

Ruby hopped from foot to foot, desperate to meet a proper land-person. If this was the owner of this wonderful house then they would welcome her for sure, as it had such a strong fellowship with the mer. Ruby could just feel it. If she had ever been asked at school to draw her perfect home then this would have been it.

The garden was filled with sunshine, blinding Ruby from seeing much except for a black outline growing in size as it moved towards her. The shape was similar to her shadow so she was sure it was human. Beside this body came a smaller being with a sideways gait. Probably an animal, she decided. Well, she was the same, she had Dolph. She gave her hair a little confidence-boosting toss. Dolph was on the path in front of her, looking in the direction of the new arrivals. His ears were pricked and his tail upright as if he, too, was watching and waiting, on edge with excitement.

Squinting and shading her eyes with her hands, Ruby tried to make out if it was a man or a woman. All the mer had long locks. Ruby's had never been cut and streamed behind her when she swam or cascaded over her when she was out of the water. The approaching image was compact with no loose strands of hair billowing around it. Obviously, there was a lot about humans she didn't know. All the same, it made her feel uneasy.

She started to chew a fingernail nervously. By the time the human came through the gate, she had bitten two fingers down to the quick and was sucking madly on them. Torn between nerves and pain, Ruby didn't know what to do. The friendly greeting she had had ready disappeared. Her earlier certainty was worn down further when she tried to catch the oncomer's eye. It was one of those simple little tips her Nan had given her.

"To know someone, you must look them in the eye and not turn away."

Instead of normal eyes, there were flat, black circles. Fingers forgotten, Ruby gaped, wide-eyed in her consternation. This wasn't a person or a mer or anything that she understood. Could it be a being without a soul? Even her Nan, who knew so much, hadn't told her about such a thing. Was this a monster, like the 'hagfish of the deep', from childhood stories? Her mother would tell her that it would come and burrow into her if she wasn't good. She had been terrified. She had stopped believing ages ago but maybe there really were monsters.

"Well, hello, child," said the newcomer, with a welcoming nod while at the same time the goose honked loudly.

Dolph yipped in reply. Unable to utter a syllable, Ruby gawped at her.

"What are you wearing?" the stranger said.

"More to herself," thought Ruby, "than to me."

With a confused, questioning look, one of Ruby's hands flew upwards to the cosy garment on her head, fluttered there a moment, and then fell back down. At this point, the stranger lifted her black eyes from her face. Taking a step backwards in alarm, Ruby gasped.

"Did I frighten you? These are sunglasses," the stranger smiled reassuringly as she spoke.

Ruby nodded, mouth open, incapable of speech. Behind the glasses were vivid, burning crimson eyes. Almost everyone she knew had blue eyes; the palest turquoise to a deep aquamarine. Nan had been one of the exceptions with hazel-brown flecks in her eyes. A quarter of one of Ruby's eyes was a hazel-brown and this had always marked her out as different. She had a habit of tilting her head to the right when talking to people so that they wouldn't comment on the hazel bit in her left eye. No one at school noticed any more or went on about it, thank goodness, but she still stood sideways on. Red eyes were shocking, though.

Too unnerved to move or think, Ruby could neither turn her head away nor blink. The vague ideas she had formed when standing in the room upstairs about her first meeting with a human were not this! The woman was relaxed and welcoming while keeping her gaze firmly on Ruby. Feeling awkward and self-conscious, Ruby's shoulders slumped and she lowered her head. Only then did the woman speak.

"I am Granny G. You had better come into my cottage and tell me everything."

Ruby shut her mouth but remained where she was, stunned and speechless.

"Follow me," said Granny G, sliding with difficulty past Ruby.

Meekly, Ruby did, with Dolph at her heels.

Inside, it was Granny G's turn to gasp.

"I see you have been here already. What a mess! Did you do this? Did your mother not teach you not to go into other people's houses uninvited?"

She banged the basket of mushrooms on the table, making them tremble, before continuing her tirade.

"Look at the drawers! Each one has been pulled out and every single cupboard door is open. The cushions are all over the floor. Didn't you think to tidy behind you? Really. Some people."

Granny G raised her arms in the air as a sign of her exasperation.

Ruby's eyes wandered around the room. She couldn't see any difference from when she had first come in. It was still bursting with stuff and colour. She hung her head in shame, though. Being scolded wasn't what she had wanted or expected.

"Sorry," she gulped.

Her cheeks flamed a bright pink and a tear that she couldn't prevent escaping ran a path down one of them. The last ten minutes were more than she could cope with. First, she had been so excited, then frightened, and finally told off.

Granny G sized Ruby up.

"Well, I suppose if we do it together we will get this tidied up soon enough."

Relief flooded through Ruby and she set to, helping Granny G put all the bits and bobs straight again. Dolph had returned to his place in front of the stove.

When they had finished, Granny G smiled warmly at her.

"Come and sit down here and tell me everything while I cook some mushroom soup. You have a hungry look."

Soon, the smell of frying mushrooms rose into the room. It was so new to Ruby that she could feel herself getting dizzy as the aroma filled her head and drifted into her empty, complaining stomach. To start with, Granny G asked questions but Ruby was too tired for more than simple answers, so they lapsed into silence.

Granny G seemed to blur in front of her but at long last she was given a bowl and plate. On the plate was a golden-brown stone. Ruby couldn't resist touching it but she must have pressed too hard because it bounced off the plate and onto the floor, leaving crumbs behind. Ruby froze. She didn't know how Granny G would behave. Would she be cross? Ruby couldn't bear her to be cross.

Fortunately, Dolph came to her rescue. He had been sitting at her feet with his tongue hanging out, panting. When she glanced in his direction, he wagged his tail. As quick as a sailfish gobbling squid, Dolph was on the stone and gulped it down in one. By the time Granny G sat at the table, it had gone.

Raising one eyebrow in a quizzical way, she eyed Ruby's plate.

"Hungry, were you? Would you like another roll?"

"Yes, please," said Ruby, in her politest tones, as she had been taught.

Sitting opposite her, Granny G picked up her spoon and said, "Tuck in."

Watching, Ruby gripped her spoon in a tight fist and tried to copy. She didn't want Granny G to think that she wasn't human. Her first spoonful was almost empty halfway to her mouth. Worried, she looked at Granny G, who nodded at her before leaning over her bowl so her face was just above it.

Dropping her own head down, Ruby was then able to slurp the soup up. Before she knew it, the soup was gone.

"I do like a girl who eats up my mushroom soup. Would you like another helping?"

Ruby nodded with a first, tentative smile. After the second bowl, she began to relax, managing a grin and a "Thank you."

"Well, I'm glad that you are feeling better. And now I think it would be a good idea if you had a bath".

"A what?"

"It's water and it gets all the dirt off when you rub hard, which you will have to do."

Ruby followed Granny G's eyes as they travelled to her mud-splattered legs.

"Oh."

"Oh, indeed," Granny G's eyebrow shot up slightly alarmingly.

Ruby wasn't quite sure what to make of it. Granny G led the way up the stairs with Ruby behind her. She felt like a little girl again, taken care of and cherished. It was wonderful and the anxiety of the last day lifted. She had been the same, once, during an illness. All the fight had gone out of her and she had done as her mother said without arguing.

The steam coming from the water as it gushed into the tub would have alarmed Ruby a short while before but now she stood and did what Granny G told her.

"Come downstairs when you are ready," said Granny G, reassuringly.

Alone in the bathroom, Ruby carefully touched the surface of the bath water where it was suspiciously calm. Her finger sent small ripples out which stilled quickly. It both was and wasn't the sea as she knew it. Tasting it left her confused as there was no salty depth to it. It was so clear and silent that with great caution she pulled the dress over her head and stepped into the tub. Immediately, her body shuddered. The water felt, oh so comforting, so warm, so wet.

She pretended she was floating. The joy of letting go, of allowing her body to unwind as it was supported by the wet embrace, was the most delicious feeling Ruby knew. When she was off jaunting with Nan, the two of them used to do it together. Nan had shown her how to empty her mind and give her whole self over to the moment. At home when she needed time to herself, she would bob on a current in the shape of a star, every muscle in her body relaxed. It was a fine way to escape from all the tension of her day at school.

Closing her eyes, she cleared her thoughts to forget everything except the float. Sadly, the bath was too cramped and her body kept knocking against its sides. The water lacked buoyancy so she repeatedly sank to the bottom. Trying not to get upset, she concentrated on emptying her mind. Pulling her head under, she opened her eyes so that the ceiling above wobbled.

"Burble, burble, swoosh, swoosh, lep, lep, ssh, ssh," went noises in her ears.

"Go away. Leave me alone," she thought, but they didn't.

They got stronger and, if Ruby wasn't mistaken, there was more than one vibration.

Spluttering, Ruby sat up. This water wasn't like the sea. She couldn't breathe in it for long. Had the funny buzzing been make believe? Under she went again and this time she heard two voices really clearly.

"Psst, psst. Wake up."

The hushed, demanding command came from a boy.

"Not now, Finn."

The girl's voice was heavy with sleep.

"Did you see it, Sylvie?"

"Didn't you hear me? I said not now."

A noisy yawn followed.

"Listen to me – did you see what happened? Sylvie, wake up."

The boy was getting more urgent.

"See what? I was … *am* sleeping."

"You sleep too much."

"So! What else do you think there is to do? What do you want, Finn?"

She gave a resigned sigh.

"Another mer child came today."

He sounded quite full of himself, giving this piece of news.

"What!"

The girl was fully awake now.

"I told you to wake up."

"I'm awake now. Tell me what happened."

"Well, as I was saying, someone new arrived and she wasn't alone!"

69

"A new person and not alone? Oh, Finn, who was with her?"

Now the girl had an eager, desperate edge to her questions.

"An animal, it came near...."

The boy was slowing down, eking out the attention.

"What animal?"

"I don't know, Sylvie."

"Okay, never mind. Go on."

"Well, it sniffed near me and scratched ..."

"Sniffed?"

"You know like this, sniff, sniff ..."

The rest of what they were saying was lost on Ruby as she surfaced for air again. There was a boy and a girl, she had been able to tell that much. Who were they and what were they talking about? Was it about her and Dolph? It was very peculiar. They had appeared to be mer but she was far away from the sea, so they couldn't be. The water was turning cold but she had to listen in one last time. Someone else joined in.

"What are you two talking about?"

There was a sharp, prying note to this girl's tones.

"Nothing."

"None of your business."

Both the first girl and boy replied dismissively.

"Well, you'd better be quiet in case anyone hears you. I don't want to get into trouble."

This was sung in a high-pitched, tell-tale way.

Ruby knew this kind of expression. She had heard it from the girls who hung around with the 'in' girls, never quite belonging but being extra mean to try and score points to raise their own status.

"We are already in trouble, Cliona."

Ruby recognised this as the girl called Sylvie, speaking as if she was explaining something patiently to a young child.

"Trouble! Hard to avoid here," the boy mocked.

Then he and Sylvie started to laugh.

"Finn, Sylvie! Don't talk and don't laugh."

This last command, coming from the girl called Cliona, rose up to a petulant squeak at the end.

After that, there was silence.

Slowly climbing out of the bath, Ruby shuddered involuntarily but not with the cold. She wasn't sure why. There was something really odd about those unusual, whispered conversations. What was it? It niggled in the corners of her mind but evaporated when she tried to catch it. Her skin smelled different and was soft in a way it had never been before. The underlying crust of salt which had always lived on her was gone.

Standing, drying herself as she had been told, Ruby felt naked in a new, vulnerable way; stripped of the sea and her merness. Granny G had laid some clothes for her on a chair and she rushed to put them on and cover herself up. The task soon took on a life of its own as she became absorbed with working out how to put them on. She hadn't really listened to the instructions and now she had to sort it out for herself.

Wriggling and squirming, she finally managed trousers and a tunic top. Very satisfied with her efforts, she was about to leave when she spotted her bag. She had to have her bag with her. The mirror wasn't in it anymore but the habit of secrecy and safety remained. With a struggle, she looped it over her shoulder and tucked it in under her clothes.

By the time she made her way down the stairs, she told herself that the mer voices weren't real but had been made up by her over-agitated mind. In the kitchen, Granny G was shuffling busily about. Hearing Ruby come into the room, she opened her arms wide for a hug. Her red eyes shone with warmth.

"Come, child," she crooned. "Did you enjoy your bath?"

"Yes, thank you." Ruby beamed up at her.

How silly she was to have felt ill at ease. She dismissed it as her imagination playing tricks. Granny G was looking after her like her own Nan would have. It was great to be somewhere she belonged and was wanted.

Chapter 10

"Come and have some of my tea," Granny G coaxed, as she placed a solid copper kettle on the stove.

"Okay," replied Ruby.

She wasn't sure what 'tea' was and whether she wanted some or not but felt that it would be rude to say no.

"This is my own special brew. Would you like to help me with it?"

Lifting a teapot down, Granny G searched in a drawer before producing Ruby's hat and putting it beside the teapot. Ruby's eyes were round with curiosity.

"Yes, what do you want me to do?"

"Did you notice the dark-leafed plants near the path when you came in, dear?" Granny G bustled about in a friendly way as she talked.

"Oh, yes, the ones that smelt so delicious?"

At last, thought Ruby, here was a task she understood and could do.

"That's right, that's them. Well, go and pick some of the leaves for me. Fill this pot."

"Alright."

Feeling more at ease, Ruby took the pot and went outside into the garden. The cockleshell path was hot underfoot and the smell from the plants rose up like a sweet, heavy mist. The red stems made an intriguing pattern against the pale path. Red on white. The colours meant something to Ruby but again, whatever it was hovered on the edge of her mind, escaping her. Distracted, she filled the pot and then stood to gaze out at the flowerbeds. She couldn't resist straying from her task to wander among them but not without furtively glancing at the house. Ruby didn't want to do the wrong thing and get told off again. Surely Granny G wouldn't mind if she stole a peek.

As she moved between the flowerbeds, she could see clearly how they had been planted individually. Each one was a boy or a girl and was unique as if they were actual people. She lightly caressed the tops of the flowers as she passed. It truly was most peculiar how real they seemed, like sleeping mer children.

"Only Granny G could have created a garden of such beauty and life," she thought.

Turning to go indoors, she noticed Dolph's tail sticking out past one of the flowerbeds.

"That's where you are. I've missed you, Dolph. What have you got there? Oh no! It's the ammonite fossil. How did you get that? Never mind. Just give it to me."

Bending to take it from Dolph, she was greeted with a low, firm growl. He placed his front paws over the fossil and bared his teeth at her. Snatching her hand away, Ruby stood, confused and hurt, when an incessant whistle cut through the air. It grew louder and louder.

"Have you got those leaves yet? The water's boiling," came a call from the house.

"Yes," her voice broke. "Yes, I'm coming."

With a last, sad look at Dolph, she turned slowly towards the kitchen. With the back of her hand, she wiped a tear away. Dolph was her friend. They were together. Why would he growl at her like that? Ruby was well-practised at covering up her true feelings to avoid the taunts of the other girls so she put on her 'hiding everything' face and went back into the cottage.

"There you are. Now, you drink this down and you will feel much better."

So saying, Granny G poured hot water over the leaves. The scent rose, enveloping the room and all within it.

"What is it?" said Ruby, opening and shutting her eyes as they stung.

"It is the chocolate flower and, like chocolate, it is warm, soft, and comforting. Drink up."

Ruby watched as Granny G stirred the cup in an anti-clockwise direction and then copied her. Blowing on it, Granny G took a taste and so did Ruby. Except that Ruby's was more of a large slurp and the hot tea burnt her lip.

"Ow!" she cried out, nursing her mouth with her hand and trying to hide her surprise.

Granny G ran a cloth under the cold tap and then passed it to Ruby, indicating that she should place it against her mouth.

"Blow first, then small sips."

Granny G showed her how to do this carefully. Very cautiously, Ruby tried again. A little trickled down her chin which she wiped away with her sleeve. This time, the drink melted on her tongue. Concentrating hard on not dribbling, she swallowed sip after sip until the cup was empty. The warmth started at her toes and spread its way up to, then along, her arms to the ends of her fingers. To her delight, she could almost feel herself floating. She had become free and easy. A tiny bubble of laughter escaped her, followed swiftly by a burp.

She looked straight at Granny G to see whether she was going to get a cross word or not. You could never tell with grown-ups. One minute, they could be kind and fun and the next, the fun was all over. She had learnt to tread carefully, especially with new people.

She wasn't going to be able to stop. She knew it. It was the same as the hysterical giggling fits she'd had as a child. She could feel them growing inside her like a balloon. For a second, Ruby swayed on the edge of mad giggles and fear of ruining her new-found happiness but then Granny G let out a large burp, too. Mischief crinkled round Granny G's mouth and eyes and then she gave a chuckle. To Ruby's amazement, it burst into the room and before she knew it, she was crumpled up with uncontrollable laughter. Granny G joined in and was soon banging her hands on the table in her mirth. The hilarity filled the previously quiet room and bounced off the walls.

The louder they laughed, the more hysterical Ruby became. Cramp doubled her over as she wrapped her arms around her body but still she couldn't stop. Neither could Granny G. When they looked at each other, it bubbled up again.

"Yip, yip," went Dolph, running into the room and jumping around Ruby, as if delighted to see her.

"Oww!" she cried, pushing him off and bending down to rub her leg where his claws had scratched her.

Still feeling hurt by his growl and guilty about the ammonite fossil, she withdrew slightly from him. Her all-consuming laughter stuttered out and in the descending silence, she felt ill at ease until Granny G furrowed her brow in concern.

"Come, Ruby, let's sit down. I'll take care of Dolph for you."

Ruby looked from Granny G to Dolph and back again. She reached a tentative hand to Dolph. She couldn't bear not being friends with him but Granny G took it and led her to the sofa. Dolph beat a hasty path through the front door before it shut behind him.

Snuggling Ruby up on the soft sofa, Granny G sat close by in her wing-backed armchair. Patting Ruby's hand, she said invitingly, "Tell me all about it."

And Ruby did. All her unhappiness gushed out. Once she started talking, she found she couldn't stop. Tales of how she hated it at school and how the girls didn't include her.

"I feel so alone," she repeated, over and over, between her stories of school and home.

She could hear her own voice moaning but didn't seem to be able to stop it. She even told about Eric being too above her to play anymore and losing Nan. A creeping sense of disloyalty crept into her thoughts but she brushed it aside quickly.

She didn't say that she had come from the sea and hadn't had legs until a day ago. There was no way to explain that without Granny G thinking that she was bonkers. Granny G listened so attentively that for the first time in ages, Ruby felt as if she mattered and here was someone who was interested in her worries. The wings at the top of Granny G's armchair half hid her face so for Ruby she was a kind of shadow, except when she looked around to catch her eye. When she did, she always smiled encouragement at Ruby with a sympathetic expression and from time to time said, "Well, I never," and "Did they, indeed!" or "How awful for you," at all the right moments.

They talked, or at least Ruby did, until they were grey shapes in a shady room. The only light left came from Granny G's eyes, which smouldered in the gloaming.

Chapter 11

Upstairs, Granny G tucked Ruby in between crisp sheets and blankets. Hardly aware of her surroundings, Ruby fell instantly into a deep sleep. It was short-lived and it wasn't long before she became restless, tossing and turning.

"Dolph, Dolph," she called out, but when she greeted him, he faded away and Granny G materialised, peering at her with an unreadable expression.

Her face got larger and closer. As it did, her features altered and instead of a gentle, fine-lined lady, there grew a hooked nose, a pointed chin, and the fiercest eyes Ruby had ever seen. The eyes were so hot that they began to burn into her. Just when she was going to scream in terror, the face transformed again. Now a boy stood there with white-blonde hair and sea-green eyes, and he was telling her something. Whatever he was saying, it was in earnest. His arms flew around frantically. His face came nearer and nearer until she could taste his breath. She swallowed a waft of salty sea. Forcing herself awake and out of the dream, she knew that all she wanted was Dolph's rough fur and firm little body to hug.

Sitting up, she wiped her sweat-drenched hair from her face. Steadying her rapid heart, she stayed as still as she could, listening to the night-time grumbles and snores of the sleeping house. Her hearing was heightened and everything sounded close and loud. She had no idea how many minutes passed as she sat there but was aware that she was holding her breath. She let it out slowly like a whisper. After a while, her eyes became accustomed to the shadows in the room. The sky was high and empty of clouds, allowing the almost-full moon to light up the floor in front of the sash window.

"What am I afraid of?" she wondered. "It's only that all this is so new and I'm in a strange place."

"I am so lucky," she decided, letting some of the fear evaporate. "Granny G is so kind and makes me feel as if I belong and am wanted. Laughing together was so much fun."

Tucking her knees up to her chest, she relaxed into the memory. She couldn't think when she had last laughed like that. Not with her mum, who was so distracted; not with Eric, nor at school. The thought of school always pulled her mouth down. All she wanted was a best friend, someone she could rely on. Not to be alone. Making friends with Dolph was great. She shouldn't have got cross with him and didn't understand what had made her behave like that. He had only wanted to play. He must have found the fossil by accident and was having a game with it. Their row didn't matter anymore. The important thing was to find him and let him know that she was sorry.

Swinging her feet off the bed, she reached out her arms to try to feel her way to the door. This room was different to the one she had been in earlier. It was smaller. She couldn't remember climbing the stairs or noticing anything. Sleep had claimed her almost before she got into the bed.

A thick rug muffled her footsteps to start with and then she was on wooden floorboards. Going as silently as possible so she didn't wake Granny G, she felt her way past looming, monster-like wardrobes and cupboards. After stubbing her toe against one, she hopped on one foot and thought about giving up and finding Dolph in the morning, but then she knew she wouldn't be able to sleep until she had said sorry and they were friends.

Creeping on, she eventually found what she took to be the door. Touching its edges, the handle appeared smooth, cold, and round in her hand. With a firm tug, the door swung open towards her.

Pussyfooting her way forwards, she found the stairs she had clattered down before. This time, she was aware of each step she took and of every moan and groan of the house. She went carefully to be sure not to wake it. As she lowered her foot on to the last board, it creaked. Shocked, Ruby froze, not daring to move. Nothing happened so on she crept. To her great relief, the front door was ajar so she slipped through it. The night air was cool and fresh after the heaviness of the house and Ruby felt as if a huge weight had been lifted from her.

"Dolph, Dolph," she whispered, as loudly as she dared. "Where are you?"

Leaving the porch, she ventured between the flowerbeds, calling him again.

"Dolph, Dolph." She could hear her own desperation. "Where are you? I hope you haven't gone away!"

With no welcoming yip from Dolph, she sat down on a stone bench, beside a flowerbed, feeling sad. Dolph had been her ally since she got her legs and she hoped and wished that he would come back soon.

Absentmindedly, she ran her hand over the flowers then turned to look at the bed. What a shock! It was the boy from her dream. There were white flowers for his hair and the heart of the two for his eyes were sea-green, edged with white petals. In the moonlight, the white flowers had an ethereal, luminous quality. They stood out starkly. In the dream, she hadn't been able to tell that he was mer but now his tail was obvious. She walked around him to get a better look. He wasn't talking to her urgently. He was lying there, expressionless, which was, of course, all that he could do. How had he got into her dream? She leant over and held her ear close to his mouth to hear if he had anything else to say but there was just silence.

Moving around the garden, she looked at the other flowerbeds. They all depicted mer people however none seemed as vibrant as the boy and she couldn't work out why. She noticed that the flowerbed she had thought of as empty before had tiny, green shoots uncurling their necks on the well-tilled soil.

"What could this be?" she wondered.

Circling round one bed, to her joy, she discovered Dolph; nose tucked under his tail, in a ball fast asleep, he was squeezed against the wall.

Throwing herself down, she wrapped him in her arms and cried, "I'm sorry, I'm so sorry. Oh, Dolph!"

In return, Dolph gave her a loving lick on her cheek.

"Oh, Dolph," she said again, laughing as she wiped her face.

Ruby ruffled his ears in a great show of affection while he wagged his tail with gusto until they were quite restored to each other. Lying down on the ground beside him, she cradled him peacefully against her. Nodding off, she murmured into his fur, "I want to go home. It is all so strange here on the land."

She must have slept for a while because when she opened her eyes, the moon was lower in the sky and a sliver of blue-pink stretched across the horizon. Standing with her hands pressed on her back like a stiff old woman, she patted Dolph farewell and sneaked back up the stairs to her bed.

The next thing she knew was her door being pushed ajar and Granny G calling, cheerily, "Wake up, lazybones. The sun has risen and so should you."

Rubbing her eyes sleepily, Ruby made her way down the stairs and into the kitchen where it was as welcoming as it had been the night before. She took a long stretch to wake up and there in front of her was Goose, his neck extended. She had forgotten about him.

"Ahh-honk."

He was still a surprise this morning. Startled, Ruby turned to Granny G, who gave her a crinkly-eyed smile while putting a bowl of titbits on the floor for Goose.

"How did you sleep?" Granny G asked, considerately.

With her hair sticking up at odd angles, Ruby covered a yawn with her hand before nodding. "Fine, thanks."

Granny G was busy stirring a pot. Her hair was loose and she seemed more normal to Ruby, more mer. Granny G's hair was pure white. Left loose, it tumbled over her shoulders to her feet, shimmering like a waterfall.

"Sip this," she said, passing Ruby some more of the chocolate plant brew.

Pouring porridge into two bowls, Granny G turned to Ruby.

"Now, how did you come to be here, lost and alone."

Concentrating hard on her bowl, Ruby wondered what to say. How could she tell the truth? And where was Dolph this morning?

"I ... I followed Dolph."

A slight tightening of Granny G's mouth was almost unnoticeable yet Ruby could hear a tinge of impatience for the first time.

"Tsk. You need to let me know where you are from if we are to find your people. I'm trying to help you."

"I don't remember." Ruby raised her gaze and met Granny G's eyes full on.

"You don't remember?" Granny G repeated each word one by one, pointedly.

"No," Ruby warmed to her story. "I woke up on the beach beside the sea. Dolph found me there and when we got to the top of the cliff, there was your house. It was so pretty and sparkly that we came here. I don't know who I am."

Pleased with herself, Ruby spoke faster and faster.

"But you must have something that will give you a clue. Did you have anything with you that might help us work it out? Anything at all, it doesn't matter what."

"This is all I have," said Ruby, wriggling her bag free from where it was hidden under her clothes.

Grabbing it, Granny G emptied the contents of the bag onto the table saying, "Good."

Out spilled the razorbill shells and seaweed in a wet, ugly clump. They sat there in a stale-smelling, green puddle that began to sink into the table. Granny G's brow darkened and her eyes became clearer and sharper.

"Rubbish! There is nothing here," she said, slamming both hands down on the table.

She turned her back on Ruby in an effort to dampen her boiling anger.

"I don't see any of this helping us. Drink your tea or it will get cold. Did you go anywhere or meet anyone before you came here?" Granny G's teeth were gritted as each sentence was hissed through them, although she finished with her mouth upturned in an empty smile.

"No." Feeling stung, Ruby's answer was shorter than she intended.

"Are you sure? Think carefully, dear." Granny G turned her charm back on.

"Well, Dolph. I met him."

"Yes, yes we know about that. What else happened on your way here? Did you stop somewhere for the night?"

"Just on the path. It got dark and Dolph and I lay down."

"Could you have lost something on the way?" Granny G's eyes scorched into Ruby as she asked this.

They were so intense that Ruby's spirit shrank into a small, fearful thing inside her.

Hesitating for a moment, she said, "I don't think so."

She stumbled over her words. She couldn't mention the mirror. Not even to Granny G, who was looking after her. A promise was a promise.

Granny G paced the room, tapping the tips of her fingers together.

"Well, well," she said. "Take the dog for a walk, follow the path you came here by. I think that you might have dropped a token from your past on the way. Remember to be back by nightfall."

Turning the full force of her personality on Ruby, she added, "We don't want anything to happen to you, do we? It isn't safe out after dark."

Ruby bit her lips together. She wanted to ask what she was to search for and pretend that she didn't understand, but there was a steeliness in Granny G's command. How could she know that she, Ruby, wasn't being completely truthful?

"I'll see if I can find something," she volunteered.

"Good girl. Come here and let me show you this."

Granny G led her to the shelf with the treasure on it and with a sweep of her hand, presented it to Ruby.

"Do you see these treasures?"

Ruby nodded.

"Well, they are the best and most precious bounty from the ocean and they were given to me as gifts. Presents, they are, for my kindness."

"Oh, yes, they are very special."

Letting her eyes run over them, Ruby spotted that the ammonite fossil was still missing. She half glanced up at Granny G to see if she had noticed its absence. As she did, her heart knocked loudly in her chest. Would Granny G notice? If she did, would she blame Ruby?

She prayed silently to herself, "Please don't let me get in trouble and be thrown out, please, please."

Not wanting to catch Granny G's eye, she nervously stared at her feet and there was the fossil on the floor, half hidden by the dresser. It would all be all right.

"Is this one?"

She reached down to pick it up and place it back on the shelf, hardly daring to catch Granny G's eye. Granny G swiped it from Ruby.

"How did it get there?"

Her eyes narrowed accusingly.

"I'm so sorry, I picked it up yesterday and can't have put it back. It felt so good in my hands. It isn't broken or anything."

"Dolph must have left it there," thought Ruby, mightily relieved.

Feeling so much easier, she found the courage to look straight at Granny G and experienced a moment of confusion. Granny G hovered between her sweet, old-lady self and something else. Something bigger, scary, and colossal with anger, before shrinking back into her own shape. Ruby blinked. Had that really happened? Again, she decided it was her imagination.

"Well, at least it is safely where it belongs now but these are not toys for you to play with, Ruby. Do you understand?"

"Yes, Granny G," said Ruby, obediently.

"Now get dressed. Then you can retrace your steps the way you came to see if you can find a present for me."

With her hands on her hips, there was a teacherly bossiness to Granny G. Ruby hurried upstairs to do as she was told. Maybe she would have to find the mirror and give it to Granny G. She didn't have anything else to offer and didn't want to fall out with her. Leaving the house, she found Dolph waiting at the door and together they set off.

Down the path they went and through the rattling gate. Ruby didn't dare look behind her at the house. She could feel Granny G's eyes fixed on her back as she walked away. She didn't know where she was going or how to find the tree.

Chapter 12

It was another bright day as Ruby walked purposefully away from the cottage with Dolph at her heels. She hoped she was going in the right direction. For a moment, a cloud blocked out the sun, making Ruby shiver. Then it shone again, bathing Ruby and Dolph in its promise of a carefree day. In spite of being watched, Ruby couldn't help having a little spring in her step on such a lovely day. Swinging her arms, she began to feel her confidence return. As she headed into the woods, she felt grateful for their shady embrace.

Dolph kept himself busy exploring the smells on the ground. He must have nosed out a mouse, rabbit, or other creature because he gave an ear piercing "yip" and was after it. Ruby was too late to see what it was but glimpsed a white spot bobbing up and down as it raced off. She whooped in delight and chased them both to the foot of a large tree where there were holes in a sandy bank. Tracks no bigger than her thumb, of a sharp-toed animal, covered the soft earth.

Peering in, she said, "Do you think we could live here, Dolph?"

Looking eagerly at the hole, he whined in reply while his tail wagged energetically.

The day stayed fine and Ruby spent it mooching about in the woods. She played with Dolph and whiled away hours, watching insects scurry under the leaves. They would run around in all directions, totally panicked, when she exposed them to the light. Absorbed in their minuscule world, she forgot about Granny G and the mirror or presents.

Late in the afternoon, she stumbled upon a tree with generous branches that looked easy to climb. Up she went until her head poked out of the top and she saw the land as far as the eye could see. The sun was low in the sky and the almost-full moon was already glowing. Searching for the familiar glint of the sea, she was disappointed. Neither could she find the arched tree although the cottage twinkled merrily. Climbing down, she became worried. As the light faded, she began to look earnestly for something to take back as a present. She didn't want to be a disappointment. There were lots of wonderful things on the forest floor. There was a spiky cone that made Ruby think of a tiny tree, which sat snugly in the palm of her hand.

"Surely Granny G would like one of these," she thought.

Hunting around, she spied one that was open and even had perfect, unbroken prongs. She put it in her bag. Spying some of the little blue flowers she had seen near the arched tree, she was certain she must be close to it. Trailing back and forth, she thought that any minute she might find it but it was nowhere to be found. Giving up, she stooped to pick a handful of the blue flowers. It felt better not to be empty-handed.

Night had fallen by the time she and Dolph reached the cottage. She dragged her feet, feeling unsure about her return. She had, sort of, looked for the mirror but was silently pleased that she hadn't been able to find it. Hopefully, Granny G would be satisfied with the cone-tree and the flowers. Then they could have a happy evening, laughing and talking like the day before. The gate rattled behind her and Dolph as they came through it, announcing their return. At once, Granny G was at the front door.

"Well?" was all she said.

In a tumble of words, Ruby said, "I looked and looked everywhere, I really did. I brought you these."

Holding her arm outstretched, she showed the flowers to Granny G. Granny G's mouth formed a thin, tight line as she took the offering and then tossed it aside onto the ground.

"What makes you think that a measly bunch of flowers is enough of a present for all my kindness?"

Her words came out flat with suppressed contempt.

Inside was no more welcoming. A single slice of bread lay on a plate for Ruby with a mug of chocolate tea. Granny G watched over her while she drank it and then went outside to talk to Goose. Her tone was soft and kindly with him. Listening in, Ruby wanted those words to be for her but instead felt isolated. Dolph hadn't come into the cottage so she didn't even have him for company. It was uncomfortable being in the house on her own and she didn't know what to do. She couldn't bear it. She ached for it to be like it had the night before; carefree and fun. If she was stuck here forever then Granny G had to be her friend. She would have to find the mirror. Tomorrow morning, she and Dolph could start the search again. This time, she'd come home with it. She imagined Granny G's surprise and delight when she handed it over. Then they would have such fun again and everything would be perfect.

Feeling happier, she wandered over to the shelf to look at the treasures. Picking them up, she was struck by how rich and detailed they were. Her narwhal handle mirror was just as unusual, maybe even more so. Rolling the ammonite fossil in her hand, she was startled from her thoughts by Granny G's voice.

"I don't know what you have been doing but you are filthy. Go and have a wash."

In spite of the harsh way Granny G spoke, Ruby didn't let it upset her as much as she might have. She had her secret and tomorrow it would all be better. In the bathroom, she struggled to remember how the water had got into the tub but with a little experimenting, managed to run a deep bath. The room was obscured with steam as Ruby stepped into it, sloshing water over the edge and letting it puddle on the floor. The water felt relaxing, more like an embrace than the night before, since there was twice as much of it. Now that she was alone and didn't have to pretend to be anyone or anything, a tear or two of self-pity crawled down her cheek.

"I wish I could go home," she thought.

Questions raced around her head. Would her mum have noticed and be worried? Would Eric be bothered about where she was? Bet he regretted leaving her out now. Would her dad be looking for her? Maybe they had organised a search party. What if they decided that she had gone, like Nan, and was never coming back? Even worse, they might stop looking! Finding her was impossible! Perhaps she should have stayed on the beach. It was too late for that. She was here with Dolph and Granny G. There was no going home.

Saddened by this thought, she pulled her head down until it was covered by the water. Breathing was more difficult today and she came up quite quickly. Was she becoming human and losing her mer blood? She had always breathed in the sea.

Back under the water, she wailed in mer, "I want to go back to the sea!"

She was greeted by a jangle of voices all talking at once.

"Me, too."

"So do I."

"Yes, help us."

"Who are you?"

"Mer."

"We are mer like you."

"But how?"

"Trapped. We are trapped."

"I don't understand. Where are you?"

"In the garden."

"Yes. Outside. We are in the flowerbeds."

"Shh, the rest of you. Stop talking all at the same time. She can't understand."

This last voice was the boy.

"Wait."

Ruby surfaced for air. The voices had a pleading, desperate note to them. They needed her, Ruby.

"Okay, I'm back."

"I'm Finn. You've seen me."

"The boy with the blonde hair?" she
guessed.

"Yes."

"How are you talking to me?"

"I don't know. We only hear you sometimes."

"Maybe it's when I'm in the bath."

"Don't have a bath."

"Why not?"

"Like you, we got legs and became lost on the land, found our way here, and now we are stuck."

"What!"

"She will try to trap you, too. Don't give her a present and don't drink the tea," his voice was urgent and beseeching.

"I feel bad not having anything for her."

"No, no. Don't feel bad. I must go."

Ruby rose out of the water and took a big gulp of air. Her fingers were wrinkled and so were her toes. This was new and strange. Her skin was smooth, fresh, and salt-free. She licked it. It tasted of chocolate like the tea. Her mind was crammed with different ideas and images.

Who was that boy? He had looked surly in her dream. Why not give Granny G a present? She had opened her home to her, and what had the boy done? She smelt the chocolate flavour of her skin again. It was sweet. So delicious that she thought she really ought to have some more. What nonsense that there were real people in the flowerbeds. A picture formed in her head of telling Granny G about it and the two of them laughing at the silly dream. Then Granny G trusting Ruby again and forgetting all about the present. That was the answer! Feeling restored and armed with a kernel of hope, Ruby dressed and went downstairs.

Granny G was waiting for her, all motherly kindness, when Ruby entered the room.

"Come and sit down, dearie," she said. "Look at you. You look more as if you are a little girl every day. I always wanted a little girl of my own."

Relief at these words ruffled Ruby like a gentle breeze. Her face lit up with innocent joy. Granny G passed her a cup of chocolate brew and Ruby sipped it. Its silky smoothness radiated through her and she patted her tummy in satisfaction. The words about the boy and the funny conversation in the bath were on the tip of her tongue when Granny G started to brush out Ruby's long hair. It hadn't been properly brushed in ages and was tangled knot after tangled knot which tugged her head. Ruby forgot about the boy as her eyes pricked with pain.

"Tomorrow you will bring me my present and today... today we will cut your hair."

"D ... do we have too?" stammered Ruby.

Cut her hair? She had no idea it was something that could happen. Why? Ruby recoiled with incomprehension at the thought.

"Yes, we must. If you are to be my little girl then you cannot have nasty, long hair, full of knots."

So saying, Granny G pulled a huge pair of kitchen scissors from a drawer and started to hack at Ruby's hair. It was so thick that it made a sawing noise and took a while to chop through it. Hot, silent tears of shame and horror coursed down Ruby's face. Reaching a hand to touch it, she found her hair stopped just past her shoulders in a ragged, torn mess. She felt light-headed as if she would float away, but her heart was as heavy as a stone. Hair lay all over the floor.

"Pick that up and chuck it on the fire," said Granny G.

Ruby obeyed her. Soon, the smell of burning hair filled the room.

"There, that's better. Now, there's no need to cry. Finish your drink."

Granny G went over to the stove and stirred a large pot before sprinkling some herbs into it. She hummed while she did so. Ruby sat still, weaving her fingers together in anguish until Granny G called her to eat. She really was an outcast now, a lost and homeless person with nobody who cared about her. She could never go home without her hair.

In bed, Ruby stifled her gulping crying by biting her fist until she dropped off. Her sleep was fitful and full of images that had her tossing and turning. When morning inevitably came, Ruby dragged her weary body downstairs to be greeted by the habitual warm welcome.

"You look just like a normal little girl today. Off you go then, poppet, go and get me my present."

Chapter 13

Dolph was waiting outside for Ruby and for the second morning they headed towards the woods. It was as gloriously warm as the day before but Ruby didn't notice. Without her hair, she felt completely lost. What would her mum say? Or Nan? It was the only time that Ruby was glad she wouldn't see Nan. Nan had had the longest, thickest hair of anyone with streaks of white running through it. She couldn't go home to the mer world like this.

The girls at school would totally mock her. If they had been bad in the past, they would be horrid now. Ruby already knew the sting of them, sniggering behind their hands and ignoring her. They would cast her out completely and forever. Overwhelmed with self-pity, Ruby sobbed afresh as she tramped along. She wasn't really sure where she was going and was surprised to find that somehow she had arrived at the top of the bay.

How had she got back so quickly? There was the sea, the blue-green sea. Boom, went the breakers crashing on the strand, and boom again. Oh, the sea. The wonderful, vibrant sea. She had missed the sound of the waves, the smell of the spray, and the surf ebbing and flowing. Scrambling down in a headlong pelt, she ran towards it, arms open wide. No friend could have been greeted with such happiness. Dolph urged her on with little yips of pleasure.

Throwing her clothes aside, she plunged into the water. The cold made her take a sharp breath but she splashed on in, jumping and whooping in her delight. The paradise of a salt wash was pure joy. The tide was coming in so she sat in the shallows, letting it cleanse her, feeling at one with herself. The gulls called crazily, both in the sky and on the rocks. Her salt-encrusted skin felt good to her.

"This is me," thought Ruby. "I must go home to the sea."

As the sun started its downward descent, Ruby realised that, reluctantly, it was time to return to the cottage. When her tail hadn't reappeared as she'd wished, hoped, and imagined, she had thought of running away but didn't know where to go and Granny G had said she was to go back. She could sense the trouble she would be in if she didn't do as she was told. Scuffing her feet, she meandered along the beach, trying to delay the moment when she had to turn and walk away from her known world.

Her eye was caught by something in the sand. She bent to pick it up. There were three or four pieces of smooth-edged blue, similar to pebbles. Holding it to one eye, everything became wobbly and the trees, the sand, all were tinged a deeper colour. It was beautiful. She had never seen anything like it. It was a treasure, a present! Relief flooded through Ruby. At last, she had a fantastic gift for Granny G. It wasn't the mirror but it was unusual. Cheered up by her find, she set off at a brisk pace. Maybe now she could tell Granny G about having had a tail and being mer. Then, hopefully, Granny G would help her find a way to get home to the sea. Lost in happy daydreams, she hummed a tune as she skipped through the trees.

Long, dark shadows wavered on the ground as Ruby reached the cottage. She and Dolph looked like tall, thin giants. She was quiet and tired now. On her way back, she had half-heartedly searched for the arched tree but hadn't seen it. She had scoured the woodland floor as well, imagining that the mirror might, somehow, be there. It made her feel better to keep scanning the ground for it; after all, it was what Granny G had told her to do and she didn't want to lie. During the day, the boy, Finn's words kept echoing in her mind.

"No present, no tea, no baths," he had said.

Well, she felt much stronger, coated in salt as she was. Maybe he had a point. Still, she clutched her blue pebble tightly. She hadn't found the mirror and a large part of her was glad.

Rushing past the rattling gate, she burst through the door.

"Granny G!" she shouted.

Two faces greeted her arrival. Sitting cosily beside the fire with Granny G was a girl. Her eyes were close together and she peered down her nose at Ruby in a haughty, unwelcoming way.

"Oh," said Ruby, taken aback.

This girl had the same supercilious air as some of the girls at school. It was as if she knew something that Ruby didn't and never would. The small amount of bravado that Ruby had gathered during the day started to retreat back to the shore, leaving her alone. She surreptitiously scanned the room for Dolph's reassuring presence but there was no sign of him.

Getting up, Granny G idly let her hand stroke the girl's head in a tender way. The girl smirked at Ruby.

"Well," said Granny G. "What is all this excitement about? Have you brought me what I asked you for?"

The red eyes burned down so deeply into Ruby that she felt Granny G could see inside her and read all her thoughts. Her hand reached for a length of her hair to twist around a finger nervously but came away empty before starting its journey again. As she stood there, a picture of gawky and ungainly discomfort, the girl spoke.

"What is it, Granny G?"

"A lost child needing a home, like you, Cliona." Granny G let her warmth shine on the girl.

"Where's her hair?" The girl, Cliona, shuddered, as she inspected Ruby.

Granny G ignored this comment and turned back to Ruby.

"My present. Where is it?" Her tone was syrupy sweet.

Overcome with nerves, Ruby reached into her bag and brought out the three pieces of blue glass. At that moment, she knew they were not good enough. They were not what Granny G wanted and only the mirror would do.

"I found these," she said, offering them up.

As she passed them over to Granny G, one piece slipped from her fingers and fell. It gave a 'ping' as it crashed on the stone floor, then a series of smaller and smaller 'pings' followed as it broke into more and more pieces, each skimming and rippling across the floor.

Ruby's hand shot to her mouth and she started to say, "I'm sorry. I'm so sorry. I'm so sorry."

"Glasssssss," Granny G's voice hissed out the word like a snake. "Blue glass, pretty BUT NOT a present worthy of me. I took you in and gave you a home … a home … and this is how you repay me."

"I'm sorry, so sorry," Ruby repeated, staring fixedly at her feet.

"Tomorrow you will bring me what I want or rue the consequences. Do you understand?" Granny G lifted Ruby's chin and held it tightly, pressing her nose against Ruby's as she spoke.

The cloying, chocolatey smell of Granny G's breath was sickeningly close. Ruby nodded, too afraid to move or think.

Granny G sat back down with Cliona.

Ruby overheard the words, "She's useless, stupid girl," followed by raucous cackling.

"What are you doing, hovering there behind us?" The dismissive words broke through to her.

"I'm sorry," she mumbled.

"Sorry. You're always sorry. Not that it does any good. Sweep this up." Granny G spoke sharply, her annoyance clear in every syllable.

Confused, Ruby didn't move. She didn't know how to tidy it up.

"She's a big, fat, useless slug. Show her the dustpan and brush, Cliona."

Ruby watched as Cliona crossed the room and returned.

"Here," she said, shoving the pan and brush at Ruby.

Ruby took them and began to sweep up the glass. Crawling as silently as possible, she tried not to draw any attention to herself but as she got closer to Cliona, she risked a furtive glance. The driftwood was in her lap! She had suspected it was there earlier but wanted to be certain. Putting the glass in the bin, she tiptoed to the stairs. Granny G and Cliona were still laughing together and ignored her. Downcast, she felt sure that they were whispering about her.

Upstairs in her bedroom, she went to the window and yanked the casement up. Sticking her head and shoulders outside, she took a big gulp of air. It seemed fresher and less stifling than the air inside. She hadn't noticed the difference before. In the garden, she could see that two flowerbeds were now empty. Feeling numb and lost, she sighed heavily and went to lie down on her bed. She lay there, staring blankly up at the ceiling. The mirror. She would find it tomorrow. It was the answer to all her troubles.

Chapter 14

In the beginning, the beginning of her life as a witch, the only time that counted, it had been such a night as this. A clear, midnight-blue sky, punctuated by deeply alive stars, lifted the roof off the world. The full moon cast an eerie glow, bathing her in its glory. All those long years ago, she had been a poor thing, a raw, bitter child, filled with the right amount of pure, low-down cunning and hatred with a twist of selfishness and a total disregard for others – the perfect ingredients needed to make the greatest witch.

"I hate you all!" she had shouted up at the sky. "I'll pay you back. You see if I don't!"

Banging her hands repeatedly on the sand, she made angry indentations in it where water seeped upwards, slowly filling them. How dare they chase her like that, as if she were a common thief? She clutched the hairbrush to her.

"It is mine. I deserve it."

They had shunned her and thrown her out for taking it. Horrid names like liar and cheat they had the gall to call her. Well, they had not welcomed her into their pod. What did she care about whether they approved of her or not? The narwhal handle hairbrush was hers, one of the seven treasures from the seven seas. From the moment she set eyes on it, she knew it had to belong to her. And now it did.

Beached. Stranded like a stupid seal. She couldn't believe this was to be her fate. The humiliation made her even crosser as it was their fault that she had become stuck here. There were no stories that she had heard of this happening to a mer before although this bay was shunned for being spooky and dangerous. Rumours of mer who came in and never returned were washed on the tide, unspoken but known. The current was fast and the entrance was narrow, making it a perilous place to enter. Nobody ever chose to come here and in her haste, it seemed like the perfect sanctuary. The tide was drawing back quickly. Soon, it would be too far for her to reach its wet safety. At least the sun had gone in. She had a better chance if she didn't dry out as quickly.

The huge, bright moon hung above her, casting its opal light on the beach. Frantically, she moved her body back and forth until she managed to roll onto her tummy and then pushed herself round onto her back again. It wasn't easy. Lithe and swift in the deep, she was ungainly and clumsy on the land. Trying a few more times brought her no closer to the sea. Panting after her effort, she lay where she was, staring skywards, hatred for the mer filling every pore of her sandy being.

Rocking over onto her stomach, to her utter surprise, right under her nose appeared two sequined objects. They were fabulous; iridescent blue-green, laced with ribbons, shimmered in the moonlight. She didn't know what they were, only that she wanted them. She went to grab one but it wouldn't budge. Her eyes travelled up from them to two legs and a body. A human! Half-squinting, she found herself face to toe with an ancient crone.

"Need help, dearie?"

It was a high-pitched, squeaky voice, issued from a dried-up, lipless mouth and the ugliest face she had ever seen.

"Go away, horrid, ugly thing."

"Ha, ha, ha," crowed the crone. "And leave you here to die? I've been watching you."

Saying that, the crone bent down and shoved her with surprising strength, over and over, her tail splashing against the surf but the deep continually out of reach.

"Into the sea, you moron, I need to go into the sea!"

The crone ignored her until, panting, she said, "Seven. What a lump you are! You cannot go back to the sea now. Can you, thief, liar, cheat? Now, hold on to that hairbrush and wish for legs."

She glared, narrow-eyed, at the crone, not wanting to give in to someone else's demands.

"Legs, I wish for legs," came her ungrateful utterance.

"Stand now and make three circles on the sand, like this."

The crone gave her an encouraging kick.

"Get off me, I can do it."

Flapping her hands in the air to keep the crone away, she stood up and completed the turns on shaky legs.

"Almost done," said the crone, scratching her hard on her shoulder with a sharp claw.

"Ow! What did you do that for?"

"Now you are a witch, like me," crowed the crone, and threw back her head, laughing.

The word reverberated around the bay, "Witch, witch, witch."

The witch stepped outside her cottage, the hem of her dress swishing over her bare feet. Black night bats beat their rapid wings through the darkness, dancing to their own, unknown purpose. She could feel the sea calling her. Tonight was the time for monsters and ghouls, and for the witch to renew her powers and finally conquer all.

In the depths of the cottage, the two children slept. The house snoozed with them and the strands of seaweed at their bedroom windows swayed gently in rhythm with their breathing. All was waiting for her return. Straddling Goose, she urged him on. His wings caressed the air with a steady whoosh as he flew above the tops of the tallest trees.

Landing on the milky-white sand, Goose honked once, loudly. The witch padded silently down to the water's edge and stood with the waves caressing her feet. She loved this pilgrimage back to the place of her creation as a witch and savoured every moment of her rebirth. Over the bay lay an expectant hush, disturbed only by the slap and plash of the waves sliding in and out.

Casting her dress aside, she walked into the cold, black ocean until it lapped against her chin. Pulling herself through the water, her long hair streaming behind her, she remembered her mer self. By straining her hearing, she caught the sounds of the deeper ocean on the other side of the bay.

"I am coming for you," she thought.

Tomorrow, the mirror would be hers. The certainty of it thrilled her. The mer child was broken; isolated and alone with her hair cut off, she had no choice except to bring the mirror. Once the witch had all seven treasures from the mer's Healers, her strength would grow and grow. The revenge for which she had waited so long was to be hers at last.

In the middle of the bay, she stopped to survey the land which was hers. Her excitement was mounting as she swam back to the shore to perform the rite which would replenish her power. In the foam where the sea met the sand, she turned round seven times as she had been taught. After this was done, she raised her arms to the heavens and spun anticlockwise three times. The power entered her with sparks of yellow and red energy tingling over her skin. Years ago, when she had been naught but a child, the foolish Healer had believed that she could be changed.

"We'll find the best in you," the Healer had said.

Well, nobody was better than she was but it was not what the Healer had hoped for. Here she stood, the best she could possibly be. Years and years had gone by and the witch still found this very funny. Tossing her head back, she cackled her amusement to the heavens. Nobody knew she existed, neither the mer nor the humans. She was the rarest of rare witches – a witch of land and sea.

When her part of the ceremony was finished, she called Goose over. He knew his role well and clawed her hard across her shoulder. Blood ran down her legs from the cut he had made. Now she had the mark of a witch. Her joy was complete. With Goose singing, "Haaannnh, haannh," loudly, and waddling about madly and chaotically, she beat her feet on the sand in an ecstatic, wild celebration.

Chapter 15

At some time in the night, Ruby awoke. Lying still with her eyes open, she was wide awake with no lingering drowsiness. With total clarity, she knew that she wanted to go home. Images of the day before flooded her mind. The empty flowerbed was Cliona's. She sat up. A picture of Cliona with the driftwood appeared in her memory. How had Cliona got the driftwood and why was her flowerbed bare? The boy, Finn, with the blonde hair, had told her something. What was it? She scratched her nose and the reassuring smell of the salty sea gave her confidence. The muddled turmoil had lifted and she felt more like herself, as if a part of her had been missing recently. White moonlight trickled into the room as she tiptoed to the window and peered at the flowerbeds again, hoping for answers. Empty! It was empty! There were two empty flowerbeds. She hadn't imagined it.

She went down the stairs as carefully as she could, trying to avoid the worst of the creaking steps. A weighty silence greeted her as if there was no one there. Even the slightest movement she made had the house vibrating and was followed by a listening, expectant quiet.

"I can't think in here," thought Ruby.

It felt oppressive and the urge to get outside was huge.

"It was so welcoming before. How long ago was that? Months and months," thought Ruby.

Although it was actually three days. Time on land was whipped up with noise saying, "hurry, hurry". Under the ocean, life was simply slow breathing and peace. She couldn't explain it.

The downstairs room was full of menacing shadows. Were those monsters hiding behind the furniture? In Ruby's imagination, they could have been Granny G, or Cliona, or Goose, waiting to leap at her and ask her what she was doing. Their meanness from the evening before when they made her feel alone and left out returned. She had so wanted to belong but now Cliona was here and Granny G preferred her. Tendrils of the confusion of the last few days wormed their way into her mind, making her feel anxious and unsure again.

While her eyes adjusted to the light in the room, her heart pitter-pattered with anticipation. Hunkering down into a small shape, she waited for her chance. It seemed a long distance to cover. Arms out and taking big tiptoe steps, she started to cross the room. There, radiating with life on the shelf, were the treasures. They cried to her to take them with her. She didn't want to. She just wanted to escape from the house, Granny G, and Cliona. Frozen by a moment's indecision in the middle of the room, panic surfaced. Then, grabbing the first treasure her hand encountered, she ran for the door. Once outside, she squatted down until she felt steady. Her relief at not being confronted was tremendous and she stayed there, taking large gulps of the cooler, fresher air.

In front of her, the cockle shell path glowed in the light cast by the moon, seeming paler than ever. The dark stems of the chocolate plant looked stark and stood out bold against it. Of course! Why hadn't she remembered before? White and red were the colours of bones and blood. They signified injury and death. She should have remembered as the granddaughter of a Healer! A spooky shiver ran up and down her spine. A few minutes earlier, being in the garden had seemed comforting after the claustrophobia of the house. Now it felt ominous and full of portent, as if it, too, was out to get her.

Rattled, Ruby backed away between the flowerbeds. She found herself beside the blonde-haired boy. He no longer seemed quite as vibrant as he had, the last time she had seen him. Somehow, he had faded away again. Leaning right over his face, she tried to connect with him.

"Finn," she said. "Who are you? What are you doing here? What did you want to tell me?"

No reply came. Only the merest flutter of his eyelashes showed that he might have heard her. It could as easily have been a soft breeze tickling the tops of the flowers. Those voices in the bath had wanted her help. This boy and the others had needed her, Ruby, but it was no good. She didn't know how to rescue anyone else. She couldn't even sort out her own life.

So lost in these thoughts was she that she didn't hear Dolph approach and was only aware of him because he nudged her on the leg.

"Dolph, it's you!" she cried, throwing her arms around him and giving him a big hug.

In her joy at being with him, she accidentally dropped the treasure onto the flowerbed. Sitting cross-legged on the ground, she pulled Dolph onto her lap, ruffled his ears, and stroked him.

"We have to get out of here," she whispered urgently to him.

Struggling out of her arms, Dolph placed his two front paws on the flowerbed and gave a little yip at her.

"No, Dolph, we have to go now!"

She tugged at the ruff of his neck. She didn't want to admit that she was scared. Saying it aloud or thinking it clearly would make it true and real.

"Come on," she urged him.

In spite of her need, Dolph worked his way free and rushed back to the flowerbed.

Taking solid shape was what looked like a real boy. Ruby was stunned. The flowers faded away while in their place were arms, legs, a face, and a body. The boy reached out a hand to her. He was trying to smile however he was still joined to the earth and his features were not yet fully formed. Who was he smiling at? She glanced over her shoulder in case there was someone there but, no, the smile was for her.

It was too much for Ruby. She screamed a loud, piercing scream, covering her ears with her hands and shutting her eyes. A deep frown appeared on the boy's face while his eyes scanned the garden. With every second that passed, he became more alive.

"Stop it." His voice was grainy and croaky from not being used.

But she didn't. His speech alarmed her even more.

He said it again, "Stop it."

This time, his voice was firm and true.

Flapping his hands in a panic, he was trying to force the awakening process by hauling his legs out of the flowerbed. After a huge effort, he managed to stand trembling in front of her. Gripping her shoulders firmly, he said, "Shh. Be quiet," slowly and deliberately.

Digging into Ruby's flesh was the ammonite fossil which the boy clutched in his hand. The sharpness of it calmed her down so that she opened her eyes to stare directly at him. He was no longer gripping her but leaning on her for support and his weight was making her legs buckle. She staggered and grabbed hold of his waist with both hands to stop herself falling over.

"You're r … r … real," she stammered. "The boy from my dream, I think." She paused. It was beyond belief. "Finn. You're Finn!"

"What are you two doing?" came a voice from the doorway.

Startled, Ruby and Finn dived apart. There stood Cliona, with a blanket wrapped around her shoulders. She narrowed her eyes at them.

"I'm telling on you," she spat, and disappeared into the cottage.

Ruby and the boy looked at each other in alarm before jumping up and giving chase. Ruby could hear Cliona's tread on the stairs as she made for Granny G's room.

"Granny G! Granny G!" came her breathless call.

Ruby was stronger than Finn and raced ahead. Cliona burst through Granny G's bedroom door, still calling. Ruby was a second behind her. They both stopped abruptly. The room was empty with the bed undisturbed. Granny G wasn't there.

Cliona's last cry fell flat, "Granny G."

Ruby had never been in this room before. It was larger than the other two. It felt like she was being trapped under a blanket of malice-soaked air. She clutched her neck as each breath burned her throat. She checked the stairs for Finn but he wasn't there. Cliona hadn't noticed and was shouting at her.

"Get out of here. You don't belong. Get away from Granny G. I'm telling on you."

The steady stream of hatred and rejection passed over Ruby as the room started to spin. A carousel of images passed through her mind, making her dizzy. Her leg bumped a table near the door. The things on top of it rattled and a brush fell to the floor.

"Look what you've done! You're stupid and clumsy."

Ruby believed her. She felt clumsy and awkward, as if everything she did was wrong. Somehow, she steadied the table and reached for the fallen brush. Once it was in her hand, Cliona, Finn, and the room were all forgotten. It was a narwhal handle brush. It matched her mirror. Weighing it in the palm of her hand, her head cleared. It was good. Cliona hadn't understood that something essential had altered until Ruby's gaze met hers.

"What have you got?" Cliona's tone had become wheedling.

"Nothing," said Ruby, slipping the brush into her bag while moving backwards out of the door.

Cliona didn't give up. Her voice changed from angry to petulant as she spoke.

"Thief! I know you have something. She will be so cross. It's not fair. Give it to me."

"No," said Ruby. "I haven't got anything. I'm not a thief."

Palms upturned, she showed Cliona her empty hands. Then she pirouetted out of the door and down the stairs as fast as her legs would carry her, with Cliona's nagging driving her. Gasping for air at the front door, Ruby was given an almighty shove by Cliona and fell on her hands and knees on the cockle shell path.

"Why does she want you? She's got me!"

The words rose to a higher and higher pitch as the door slammed shut behind her.

Chapter 16

A thin light was stealing through the darkness, lending a washed-out grey colour to the garden and everything in it. Sometime during the night the clouds had rolled in, bringing with them a moist warmth.

"Morning already," reflected Ruby, wearily. "I need to go home."

She didn't notice Finn, who stood, lost in thought and unmoving, beside a flowerbed. Brushing dirt from her knees, Ruby was about to head out of the gate when she spotted Dolph lying at Finn's feet. A tumble of emotions caught up with her; Cliona, boys appearing from the earth, not enough sleep, or food to eat. The last straw was Finn taking her dog. At once, she felt cranky and peevish and stomped over to him.

Arms crossed and brow furrowed, she spat, "What are you doing with my dog?"

"Your dog? I'm sorry he just sat there." Finn shrugged.

His nonchalance infuriated her even more.

"Yes, my dog. Give him back."

Then Finn laughed an amused, teasing laugh. It reminded her of Eric being too clever and impossible. She put her hands on her hips and glowered at him.

"I thought," he said, "that you would be … I don't know … different, nicer."

Just as quickly as her temper had arrived, it evaporated, leaving her feeling guilty.

"I'm sorry. I'm Ruby," she muttered, sheepishly.

"I guessed as much," he replied slowly, as if trying to work out what was going on with her sudden mood change.

"I was just leaving."

"Me, too."

Finn glanced down at the flowerbed. A girl was materialising into human form from the flowers. In her hands, she held the blue coral.

"Who is she?"

"She's my cousin, Sylvie."

He faced Ruby directly. His eyes searched hers and she could feel him taking her measure. He must have decided to trust her.

"I found the sharks tooth necklace and the sea urchin shell while you were upstairs. I have given them to Zale and Ianthe. I can't find the last treasure. Who was that girl in the house?"

Shrugging at most of the questions, Ruby looked over at the house and said in a tone of pure distaste, "That's Cliona. Don't you know her?"

"Cliona. I've spoken to her but never seen her before." Finn questioned, "Did *you* set her free?"

"No. Not likely. She was just there last night when I got back." Ruby's dislike of Cliona could be heard clearly.

"Cliona's like that. She still loves Granny G, in spite of everything."

Finn chewed his bottom lip thoughtfully. Very little of what he was saying made sense to Ruby so she took her chance to ask him a question of her own.

"Why were you all in the flowerbeds?"

"Granny G put us there. She tricked us into giving up our treasures as gifts for her and as soon as we did, we were trapped and fell into the flowerbeds."

"Really?" Ruby questioned, doubtfully.

He had spoken with sincerity but it was a very strange story.

"Yes, really," replied Finn, firmly.

"But why?" demanded Ruby.

"I don't know," said Finn, showing her his ammonite fossil, "but I think it is something to do with this."

"Is that the present you gave her?" said Ruby, as Finn shook his head sorrowfully. "I haven't given her anything. I didn't have anything to give."

"What?" Finn's mouth hung open and he stared at Ruby. "How come you are here and how did you hear us? It doesn't make sense!"

"I lost it." Ruby thought a small lie wouldn't hurt.

Even though Finn seemed truer than anyone else she had met so far, she still didn't want to tell him the entire truth.

"It fell out of my bag on my way here. I've been searching for it ever since."

Finn's eyes grew round. "She must be furious."

"Well, she has looked after me and I should give her something."

Finn was insistent, "No way! You don't owe her anything. This whole thing is a trap."

"Ahh-honk," hissed Goose, making them jump.

Next, there was an alarming clatter as the shark's tooth necklace bounced on the ground.

"Ahh-honk," came his cry, as he marched purposefully towards the sea urchin shell.

Dolph was the first to react. He rose to the challenge and started barking at Goose. Wings wide, Goose hopped and flapped away, landing on a flowerbed. The sea urchin shell lay there in all its fragility. If it were thrown, who knew what would become of the mer girl whose flower-hands it rested upon? Dolph gave chase, hackles up and tail puffed.

Still the goose came on, his long neck stretching upwards, honk-honking as he did so. Dolph leapt onto the flowerbed. With the muscles on his shoulders taut and legs spread apart, from deep within him came a threatening growl. Goose's spiteful eyes showed the disdain in which he held such a small dog. Waggling his head from left to right, he suddenly lunged at Dolph to give him a sharp bite. Ruby shouted in fright and Dolph sidestepped quickly. As she rushed over to him, the noisy commotion of the two animals split the air.

The fight was fierce and Ruby could neither grab the sea urchin shell nor help Dolph. Dolph was quick on his feet. Dipping and diving, he attacked Goose by trying to get underneath him. However, Goose was a large bird with a long reach and a dangerous beak. Bravely, Dolph managed to force Goose away from the flowerbed but only for a moment. Infuriated, Goose rose up off the ground and charged at Dolph, catching him on his side with a vicious nip. Dolph squealed in agony then stumbled and fell.

"Dolph!" cried Ruby and grabbed Goose's tail, flailing at him with her fists.

Furious at this second onset, Goose craned his neck round, beak ready for a mean pinch. Clinging nimbly onto his back, Ruby found that they were trapped in a clumsy dance together. At least their jig took them further away from Dolph and the sea urchin shell. Ruby's arms were starting to tire. She couldn't hold on for much longer and Goose was not going to stop.

Just when she was beginning to despair, the gate rattled open and Granny G made her entrance.

"What is going on here?" Her voice resonated with displeasure in the small space.

Instantly, Ruby was jolted off Goose's back, scrambling for balance. Goose's tail feathers quivered with disdain. He rearranged them, his long neck shivering with indignation. In a state of shock, Ruby started to cry; a gulping, snotty noise like a toddler in meltdown. Granny G's attention focused on her. Ruby could feel it and felt self-conscious. Her sobs slowed. There was a look of revulsion on Granny G's face as she took in Ruby's plight before expressing concern.

"What is it, child? You can tell me," she soothed.

Moving closer to Ruby, she passed her a hanky. "Everything!"

Gesticulating gently, Granny G motioned to use the hanky. Catching on, Ruby wiped her eyes and blew her nose.

Quickly, Granny G scrutinised the garden. What had been orderly was now upside down and chaotic. To her horror, some of the mer children were rising. The flowers were fading and being replaced by solid limbs and bodies. Her features began to contort and change, anger simmered at the awful truth in front of her. The red of her eyes turned a dark vermillion, her cheeks flamed, and the ugliness within her could no longer be contained. Ruby watched in awe as Granny G seemed to shrivel, then grow, and then finally settle back to normal as she gained control over her emotions. Only her eyes still burned with a mixture of greed and wrath. All at once, a new intensity entered them.

During her grapple with Goose, Ruby's bag had slipped from under her top. A handle made from narwhal horn had come loose and was sticking out tantalisingly.

Rubbing her hands together in glee, Granny G purred, "What have you got there, child?"

Her tone was honeyed and caressed Ruby with its sweetness.

Ruby hiccupped and turned a trusting face upon Granny G. Part of her still craved kindness so much, she melted under it. Maybe she didn't have to go after all.

Eventually noticing that Granny G's gaze was fixed on the handle, Ruby slowly understood what she was being asked and stammered, "I found it. It fell," she said, simply.

"Well, what a good girl you are! Bringing me a present at last."

"Oh no, it's not…" Ruby replied, suddenly realising that Granny G thought it was the mirror.

She was on the verge of passing the brush over but paused, not wanting to reveal the mistake. In that second, a new voice broke through the pseudo- intimacy.

"No!" it cried, firmly.

Appearing from a corner of the house was Finn. With one hand, he dragged his hair off his face, clearly showing the determination etched there. The other hand was held flat out as if to stop an invading horde.

"Goose!" spat Granny G.

For a second, Goose's expression said, "I told you so," before her withering stare had him cast down. He waddled to her side saying, "Wink, wink," pathetically.

"Don't do it," ordered Finn, his gaze fixed firmly on Ruby.

She wasn't sure she trusted either of them. Where had Finn been when she was saving Dolph? She backed away from them both.

"Don't trust her," he pleaded.

"What nonsense. Come here and give me my present," Granny G cajoled, holding out her arms.

Appraising one against the other, Ruby was completely undecided. She took a step towards Granny G.

"Stop!" shouted Finn. "Think of Dolph. You can't give it to her."

"Don't listen to him, Ruby, darling. Come here and give it to me at once." Granny G added a note of authority to her request.

"Poor Dolph," wailed Ruby.

"What about Dolph?" Granny G's voice couldn't quite hide the fact that she found it annoying to be diverted by the dog.

"Your goose attacked him!" Finn pointed an accusing finger at her.

As they argued, Ruby put her hands over her ears. If only they would stop fighting. She wanted to escape from them both and return to the peace of her underwater world.

Treading silently, trying not to be noticed, she retreated. Granny G didn't move but Finn advanced further into the garden. Behind him, a girl sat shakily on an empty flowerbed.

Sliding her hand into the bag, the cool smoothness of the narwhal horn lay against her hand. It could have been the mirror; it felt the same, right somehow, as if it did belong to her.

"It's mine," she sighed, more to herself than to either of them.

As she paused, both Finn and Granny G edged towards her. Finn held out his hands imploringly to her.

Granny G started to speak. "Come now, child. I didn't have anything to do with what happened to your dog, did I? You give me my present and we can go inside and forget all about this, can't we? Let's have some tea, and I have a delicious chocolate cake. You haven't tasted cake yet but you'll love it. It will be a treat. We can make up, put all this behind us, and go back to being friends again. What do you say? Don't you want to be my special child?"

Ruby's shoulders slumped down. She did want a Nan and to belong. She missed her own Nan. As she dithered, Granny G slid a bit closer.

"No, no, no! It's a trap. You can't trust her. Do you want to be the last flowerbed?"

Ruby tilted her head in Finn's direction as if she was finally awake. He was right. She was being ensnared. His gaze was steady and sure. Beside him was the girl, Sylvie. She didn't know them well but they were mer children like she was. Then her hand came to her mouth and her vision clouded over. Except not like her anymore. Not now that her lovely hair was shorn. How could she go back to the sea without it? How could she stay with Granny G, who had cut it off? She hesitated. This time, Granny G decided to negotiate no longer and lunged at Ruby. Goose, ever faithful, encouraged her with a high-pitched, piercing, "Ahh-honk."

"Come here, come here!" screamed Finn, jumping up and down.

Chapter 17

Ruby looked around her. Goose was honking like a desperate cheerleader, Granny G was grunting with the effort of trying to grab her, and Finn was shouting her name endlessly. The noises blended into a white blur of sound, spinning around her while she stood at its axis for a moment, motionless. She blinked and they all came back.

"Granny G," screamed a voice.

From the house, in a frenzy, ran Cliona. Hands outstretched, she tugged at Granny G's arm. Jabbering, her words rushed out in a long, incoherent stream.

"ShetookitIcouldn'tstopherItriedreallyIdid you'vegottob elievemeI'mthegoodgirlyou'llsee."

Granny G tried to shake her off but couldn't. Cliona's grip was limpet-like. Frustrated, she stamped her foot on the ground, sending a tremor that shook the house and children. Removing Cliona's vice-like grasp, she cast her to the ground where the girl fell, sprawling. She hadn't understood Cliona's long spiel and spat the words, "Stupid girl," in her direction.

Stubbornly, Cliona didn't give up, whimpering. "I tried to stop her. She took it."

On the point of turning her back, Granny G swivelled and focused on the words. Reaching down, she yanked Cliona by her top and half lifted her off the ground.

"What did you say?"

"Your brush. She took it. I tried to stop her. I did."

Even though she was half hanging, pirouetting on her toes, Cliona was pleased to have Granny G's full attention. Her pleading was replaced with a wheedling note.

The sight of Cliona had made Ruby's mind up. Cliona was not to be trusted and she certainly did not want to be with her.

Making the most of Granny G being distracted, she went to join Finn and Sylvie. Passing a flowerbed she noticed, in the last stages of awakening, a doleful, slender girl, holding the sea urchin shell. She was so fragile that Ruby stopped to lift her up and by half carrying her, they managed to get to the others. From the opposite direction, a black-haired boy swaggered towards them. Round his neck, he was busy fastening the sharks tooth necklace. His eyes met Ruby's and he shot her a wide, cheeky smile. To her amazement, his teeth were all pointed like the sharks teeth which gave him the most rascally appearance. It didn't help that short tufts of hair grew straight up from his head, framing his face.

"I'm Zale," he said.

Even his voice had a bold edge to it.

The girl let go of Ruby and said, "Thank you, I am Ianthe."

Four sets of expectant eyes turned to Ruby for answers.

"What now?" Finn asked.

For that instant, Ruby felt what it was like to be popular. How could she let them know that she had no idea? Before she had time to tell them, a dark shadow passed over the

125

sun. Light and warmth were blotted out. With a clamour of wings and cries of "gah-gah-gah," and "kay-ow," the sky above them was filled by an enormous flock of seagulls.

A wide-winged, black bird was in their midst, confidently leading them on. Slowly, so slowly, as if her brain had stopped working, Ruby realised that it was Goose. He had been grovelling on the ground a moment before. Her mind and body were not able to react in time to what she saw. This noisy, aggressive cloud was coming for them! Near the gate stood Granny G, her arms raised to the birds.

"Kek-kek-kek, kow-kow-kow," she sang.

Her feet hardly seemed to touch the ground, she was twirling round so fast while commanding her flock. Ruby had only ever seen Granny G dressed in dark colours but on her feet now were the most amazing shoes. Their turquoise sequins sparkled, even in the dull, early-morning light. Her hair circled around her as she spun. Her lips were deep red and she seemed more alive somehow, more vibrant. Energy coursed through her, up to the birds and outwards; she appeared younger and full of power. It was Granny G and yet it was difficult to believe she was the same person. Cowering on the ground beside her was Cliona. A slight twinge of pity for her passed briefly over Ruby and was gone. The oncoming attack drove everything else from her mind.

Whooshing down came the birds, clawed feet out and ready, sharp beaks pointed to peck. At arms-length above the children's heads, they hovered, flapping madly. At first, the children stood, open-mouthed, staring upwards in disbelief. Shrouded as they were by the dark cacophony, fear took hold of their hearts and thoughts. It left them stunned, unable to move.

A black-headed gull broke away from the crowd, descending to scream in Finn's face then rising back up. Ruby could hear it laughing with its cronies. They were being tormented, played with. She felt like the prey of the Garfish; she'd seen how they toyed with them before catching and eating them. It was cruel and horrible.

A whimper came from Ianthe whose eyes were large with horror. Zale pulled her close and held her head against his chest. Instinctively, their knees gave way and they sank downwards to the ground. Nobody spoke as they huddled together for comfort. A second bird dropped from the sky. In an instant, its claws became entangled in Sylvie's hair. The gull flapped back in a madness of beating wings, wrenching Sylvie's hair. She started to scream and hold on to her head but they were joined together. With a frenzied beating of its wings, the gull shrieked its panic. Its call unnerved the rest of the flock. In ones and twos, they broke free to dive at the children with a vengeance.

Ruby backed up towards Ianthe to offer her more protection. Finn rushed to help poor Sylvie. She was screaming wildly as her hair was pulled out. By gripping it close to the roots, he was able to reduce the tearing of her scalp. At the same time, he tried to ward the birds off by waving his other arm around. Zale and Ruby were also trying to beat the birds away but there were so many of them. The gulls nastily ripped at their faces and they were forced to cover their eyes. For a second, through a gap in the wings, Ruby caught sight of Finn's back which was covered in gashes. Her arms were becoming tired.

"Soon, they will get me," she thought.

As she crouched, hugging her knees, her bag knocked on the path. Yanking it off her and holding it by the strap, she swung it round her head. Faster and faster it went, spinning a circle in the air above their heads. The long handle sang as it whirred around and the birds backed off. They retreated, some settling on the roof of the house and others on the walls and empty flowerbeds where they continued their threatening behaviour, screeching and jumping aggressively. For the time being, they remained a wall between the children and Granny G.

"The house," said Ruby, half to herself and half to the others.

She began inching towards it. She knew that they had to get there and soon. Her arm was beginning to ache and she didn't know how much longer she could shield them. Shoving Zale and Ianthe, she tapped Finn on the shoulder and pointed. He nodded. Stooping, he picked up Sylvie and half carried, half dragged her, under Ruby's lasso of safety, to the house.

Chapter 18

Once through the door, they slammed it and collapsed on the floor, shivering with fear. The stone flagging was cold against their ravaged skin and relief flooded through them. Ruby realised that she didn't know how Sylvie had escaped from the gull.

"What happened?" she asked her, twisting a finger in a strand of hair to mime her question.

Sylvie parted her hair and showed Ruby where a chunk had been torn from her scalp. Exhausted, they stared blankly up at the ceiling, too worn out to talk. Ianthe had suffered the least, thanks to Zale, and sat cross-legged on the edge of the space on the floor which they had claimed as a den. With her sea urchin shell cradled in her hands, she bent over it until her nose was almost buried in it. Hidden by her long hair falling in front of her face, her hands, and the shell, she was deep in a world of her own. Ruby felt the stirrings of unease. What was she doing? Ianthe must have become aware of Ruby's gaze upon her because she lifted her head and gave Ruby a sweet, satisfied smile. Coming close to Ruby, she dabbed sea urchin butter on her wounds as a salve. Where a moment before had been stinging cuts and bites, there was now a cool, healing prickle.

"Wow," said Ruby, "that's amazing."

Ianthe nodded her acknowledgement and went to Sylvie to tend to her.

Feeling hungry, Ruby heaved herself up to snoop for something edible. Opening cupboard doors and exploring inside them, she didn't find anything she recognised as food. Delving into a large crock-pot on the side, she discovered two rolls. She remembered thinking that they were stones. Crushing one in her hand, she was about to stuff some into her mouth when Finn knocked it aside.

"No," he said, firmly. "We mustn't eat her food."

Ruby tossed the second roll into the crock-pot and stomped back to the others. After a mostly sleepless night, nothing to eat, and the attack from the gulls, she was cranky.

"What are we going to do?" she snapped at them all.

"We must get back to the sea," said Ianthe, in her soft lilt.

"Yes, but how?" A surge of impatience made her sound sharper than she intended. "I need to eat. I don't know what to do."

"Finn is right. We cannot eat her food. It makes you do things you don't want to. I am sure that is the way she trapped us. Can you feel the menace in the house?"

As he spoke, Zale cast an eye everywhere, as if something was going to leap out at him. The oppressive atmosphere in the house struck Ruby again. They were right; no eating or drinking in here.

"I thought you didn't have a treasure?" Finn asked her.

"I didn't," replied Ruby, biting her bottom lip.

"What was in your bag then?" There was a seriousness to Finn that she hadn't expected.

Reluctantly, Ruby replied, "I found it upstairs when I chased Cliona. I don't know. I don't understand it but I think it is mine. It worked, didn't it?"

She had everyone's attention. All eyes were fixed on her with intense curiosity. Ruby wasn't good at trusting anyone completely. Nobody asked anything else about it so Ruby decided to change the subject.

"Is Cliona one of you?"

"She is mer like us. Somehow the knot she's tied herself to Granny G with is a tight one – one that she doesn't want to let go of. Her treasure is mer made and is not as powerful as ours. I suspect that is why, anyway." Sylvie's voice was strong and steady and, if it hadn't been for her uncertainty at the end, Ruby would have thought that she was a grown-up.

"So it is just us," she said.

"No," said Finn. "There is one missing. We are seven, or six without Cliona. We must stick together."

There was a murmuring of agreement to this. Ruby wanted to be part of it but still felt like an outsider. They had known each other for longer and suffered together in ways in which she wasn't included.

"Who is missing?" Ruby asked them all.

Zale scratched his head, Ianthe stared at her hands, and Sylvie and Finn shrugged.

"Whoever they are, they never spoke. I believe they have been here the longest. Maybe they're stuck?" Finn added.

"I've seen the last flowerbed and it is a boy," said Ruby.

"We must try and rescue him," pleaded Ianthe. "We cannot leave him behind here forever. Oh, no."

131

"But there are no more treasures. They were all there on the shelf and there are none left. I picked them all up. Didn't I, Ruby?" Finn turned to her.

Ruby nodded.

"Think," said Ianthe. "Is there anything else you have seen that could be a treasure?"

"No, nothing," she replied, slowly.

A bang, followed by a resounding crack, made them jump closer in alarm. Sometimes, in the sea, there were loud 'booms' when it felt as if the world would collapse, and the noise could be so powerful that everyone cowered in fear. This was the same sensation; as if the sea was falling on their heads. There was another boom, then another, and another. The walls of the house couldn't take it and began to bow outwards.

Ruby crawled to the door and put one eye to the keyhole. Straight in front of her was Granny G. Her feet were back on the ground while her hands waved in the air, gesticulating orders to the birds. Ruby couldn't see many of the gulls; there were just a few stragglers who were being sent to the roof. The birds were bringing the house down. Granny G was going to collapse it on top of them. Shaking, she returned, wide-eyed, to the others.

"The gulls are on the roof! It isn't safe. We have to leave, right now!"

Zale put a hand on her arm and smiled his wicked grin. "Okay," he said. "Can you get us out with what is in your bag, Ruby?"

"I can try," she replied, hesitantly.

The house gave another almighty rumble, followed by a series of groans. Some plaster flaked off and sprinkled onto the floor while the ceiling lamp swayed precariously above them.

Screaming, they dashed to the door as if to escape but stopped short. Opening it a crack, Finn and Ruby peered around. Granny G was still on the path. Cliona was no longer subdued but was dancing about with glee as the house began to crumble. Little puddles had begun to form from the rain and she had been stomping in them.

"Can you see Goose?" whispered Finn.

"No," replied Ruby, although she didn't say that she was really looking for Dolph.

He had never been far from her thoughts and she had kept her fingers crossed, hoping that he wasn't too badly hurt. Trying not to attract attention, Finn was pushing the door back when Ruby shouted out, "Wait!"

"Look," she said to him, and pointed to the door.

There, on the front, was the conch shell knocker.

"That's it! It's the last treasure. It must be. It's magnificent so it just has to be special," Ruby was delighted. "I'll take it to the flowerbed."

Having something to do had released positive energy.

"I'll come, too," said Finn.

Chapter 19

The two of them slid out of the front door. Wrenching the conch shell from the door took ages.

"I can't shift it," Ruby hissed. "It's stuck!"

"Knock it with something," Finn replied, his back to the door, guarding her.

Desperately, she pulled the brush from her bag, being careful to keep it hidden from the watchers in the garden, then hit the shell with it, loosening it.

"It's coming!" she said.

At last, it snapped off cleanly. Her eyes met Finn's and they nodded at each other. Finn took the conch and Ruby clutched her bag tightly, keeping it at the ready. It seemed like small protection against an army of gulls and an irate Granny G.

Seeing them forced out of the confines of the house, Granny G gave a high-pitched, witch's laugh. Ruby froze and hesitated for a second. There was joy in that sound. She had the distinct impression that Granny G was relishing their panic and discomfort! Her gaze was reluctantly drawn to the witch. She rubbed her eyes in disbelief. Granny G had changed. The rosy glow in her face had gone and been replaced with a haughty, arrogant air. Her plump cheeks were sinking inwards and wasn't her nose bigger and longer? It unnerved Ruby so that she shuddered, electrifying the tiny hairs on the back of her neck. She swore that they sent out waves of her fear because, if she wasn't mistaken, Granny G grew taller that instant.

"I'm going mad," she thought, reaching for Finn.

Hand in hand, they darted between the flowerbeds until they found the one belonging to the unknown boy. The earth around the soil was sodden and heavy, like clay. Kneeling, Finn screwed the shell down hard into the soil, making sure it was stuck firm. Agitated that any moment now an attack was going to start, Ruby hopped about.

"What now?" she mouthed to Finn. "Can we leave him?"

Finn shook his head.

A large raindrop plopped onto Ruby's arm. Flat blobs of water spattered down, first one and then another, creating an eerie quiet. In anticipation of action, some of the gulls flew off the roof and swooped alarmingly at Ruby and Finn but withdrew before hitting them. They stood back to back for safety, scanning the garden for signs of danger. Granny G hadn't moved which was more frightening than anything else. Something was coming. All their hope rested in the comfort of each other's presence.

"Stay with me," she said, and he squeezed her hand tighter.

"Together," Finn replied.

An annoying buzzing honed in on Ruby's ear and she flipped it aside. A black and yellow insect landed on her nose, making her go cross-eyed. She jumped with fright, flicking it away but another came and then another. The constant "brrr" of wasps surrounded them, making it impossible to stay calm as it worked its way into their brains. Driven crazy trying to avoid them, they brushed their heads with their hands and ducked and dived, appearing to anyone watching as if they were performing a lunatic dance with no rhythm. More and more wasps came.

The first sting made Ruby gasp with its sharp, biting pain. An angry lump was forming on her arm. A fleeting glance showed Granny G pointing in their direction, orchestrating these evil insects. Ruby had no idea where Finn was anymore, her only thought was to escape the never-ending stings but she couldn't. Her legs, body, and arms throbbed with the bites while her ears thrummed with the infernal buzzing.

Ruby swung her bag as she had for the gulls but it just didn't work. The wasps crawled all over her so she was unable to twirl it. They were so small, she needed all her concentration to fight them. The rest of the world faded away, all that remained were these tiny, winged attackers. Although the gulls were still leaping up and down on the roof, shaking their heads at the children, and the house groaned and creaked, Ruby didn't notice.

As the house folded in on itself, it gave a last, deep rumble. Three children shot out of the front door, seconds before the collapse. They had their hands over their heads and raced towards Ruby and Finn, shouting. A distant part of Ruby wanted to warn them to go back or somewhere else but she couldn't, locked as she was in her own personal struggle.

Small pieces of shell sailed through the air, cutting intricate patterns as they did. Dust billowed skywards and obscured the gulls when seemingly by a miracle, they emerged out of the rubble, filling the air with their strident cries. The last out was Goose, who circled high, wings spread wide before dropping down to land beside Granny G.

A loud, outraged howl managed to break through the rest of the clamour and penetrate Ruby's head. Someone was hurt. Spinning in her gyrations, she tried to find out who was injured. Zale, Sylvie, and Ianthe had started their own individual insect avoiding routines. Sylvie was using her hair to defend her by pirouetting fast and letting it swirl around her. Ruby was impressed. The cry wasn't from Finn or those three.

Over by Granny G, Cliona's face had broken up into an unhappy mess of misery. Standing in front of the house, she had caught the worst of the impact. Blood trickled in rivulets down her body, arms, and legs. Granny G gathered her in, stroked her hair, and mollified her until a lopsided smile appeared on Cliona's woebegone face. Even Goose made a show of being sympathetic, waddling up close and leaning against her. Ruby stared with a quizzical look at the three of them, joined together in this unexpectedly tender scene.

"Come, child," Granny G beckoned to Ruby, reaching out her hand. "Only I can help you."

Her voice had a hypnotising quality speaking of home, and rest, and safety. Melodious and rich, Ruby heard the music of the deep ocean rolling over her, calling her, sucking her into Granny G's energy. Across the ground separating them, Ruby sensed the fiery eyes piercing through her to the centre of her being. A world of weariness lay on top of her and the urge to give in was irresistible. Surrender appeared almost inevitable. She batted a wasp away from her ear. They had lost. What else could she do?

Dropping her chin to her chest and letting her arms flop in a picture of defeat made Granny G swell to an even greater height. In a gesture of assurance, Granny G took a pin from her hair, releasing it, so that it fell in white waves over her shoulders and down to her shoes.

"Ahh-honk," cried Goose, nipping Cliona on the back of her leg in his excitement, then hanging his head in shame as Granny G glared at him.

Deep inside his cocoon of wasps, Zale was dimly aware of Granny G's growing self-belief and Ruby's hopelessness. With a great effort, he worked his way over to Ruby and stood in front of her. Determinedly, he thrust his head up and forwards and smiled his cheekiest smile at Granny G.

"Move away, shark boy." With a wave of her arm, she dismissed him.

Only then did he realise how her strength had grown; his legs buckled beneath him and gave way, leaving him kneeling on the ground as if he'd actually been hit. Crouching low, he bared his teeth at her. Ignoring him, she expanded. Finn, Sylvie, and Ianthe stopped their battles with the wasps and stilled. Their bodies showed every sign of being worn out. They were covered in raised welts and sores from the many stings they had suffered. Poor Sylvie swayed, hardly able to stand, as the wasp poison coursed through her.

"Come to me and all will be well," coaxed Granny G.

Palm up, she curled her fingers inwards, drawing Ruby in. Reluctantly, Ruby lifted a heavy foot to take her first step towards Granny G when a piercing singing broke the air. It was a haunting tune and at its sound, Ruby snapped out of her trance-like state. The wasps hated it. They zinged wildly around, bumping into each other and the collapsed building, before escaping the garden and into the woods beyond. Freed from following Granny G's instructions, they made their way back to their own lives, forgetting instantly the thrall in which they had been held.

The last flowerbed boy had awoken. Holding his conch shell to his ear, he sang. His voice was true, and rolled over, around, and into Ruby, filling her with memories of love and home. Standing, feet apart and confident, he was a tall, well-made boy.

"He's almost a man," thought Ruby, gawping at him.

Ianthe was the first to reach him. Finn and Sylvie hastened to his side where Ianthe was soon busy with her urchin butter salve. Seizing the moment while Granny G was also shocked by the arrival of the new boy, Ruby tugged Zale up and together they lost no time in joining the others.

At this unexpected turn of events, Granny G's face contorted in anger. Pointing a long-nailed, wrinkly finger at them, she said, "You, you, you, and you; I'll get you all yet."

She stamped her foot on the ground and tremors rippled out leaving cracks in their wake. A watery sniff behind her earned Cliona a sharp clip on the head.

"Stop your snivelling."

Chapter 20

In the lull, the children gathered beside the new boy and inched their way around the garden. The gate lay before them unguarded; their path to freedom, the sea, and home. Dipping her hand into her bag, Ruby let it rest on the cool, horn handle of the brush. As it always did, it cheered her up and gave her confidence. Wrapping her fingers around it, she drew it out of the bag and held it close.

As they reached the rattling gate, Ruby suddenly remembered Dolph.

Stopping, she called his name, "Dolph, Dolph."

She couldn't leave without him and panic rose in her chest. The new boy placed his hand on her arm.

"There is no time."

Shrugging him off, Ruby dashed away from the rest of the group, darting between the flowerbeds to where she had last seen Dolph. He lay, slumped and unmoving, and for a heartbeat she thought he was dead. His name caught in her throat, half said. At the sound of her voice, he raised his head and whimpered. Tears of relief coursed down her face as she knelt to scoop him up in her arms.

"Oh, Dolph," she wept.

Unbalanced by his weight, she struggled to lever herself up by balancing on the edge of the flowerbed. Once standing, she leant back while trying to adjust her hold on his body, talking to him in a calm, steady way all the time, determined to get them both out of there. The brush dug into her hand, adding to her difficulties, and she wished she'd put it away but knew there was nothing to be done now. She set off.

A furious hiss made her start and almost drop her bundle. Behind her, Goose was closing in. Ruby staggered backwards with her load held clumsily. Back she retreated with Goose advancing, neck thrust aggressively towards her, beak snapping, small eyes keen and evil. Like a confident hunter, Goose drove her on until he had her cornered. She tried to escape to one side but her feet crossed over each other and she tripped. Crying out in alarm, she landed painfully on her knees. She grasped Dolph tighter but the brush fell from her grasp.

It clattered onto the path and bounced a couple of times before coming to rest. Granny G's head swivelled at the sound. Her eyes fixed on the brush and a stillness settled over everything while the enormity of what had been exposed sank in.

"My brush!" Her voice was incandescent with anger.

It cut cleanly through the air.

"Get it, Goose!" she screeched.

Goose was nearest to it, barely a waddle away. Stretching his long neck forwards, he managed to reach it and draw it towards himself. Ruby hadn't let the brush out of her sight either but was pinned down by the weight of the dog she was carrying. Shifting his body against her own, she gathered herself into a squat and from there, to standing. Aware of her challenge, Goose glared at her, eyes full

141

of unadulterated malevolence. His hatred tingled along Ruby's spine making her shiver. He gave an "ahh-honk", warning her away. Shocked by such intense animosity, she raised her eyes to Granny G, appealing for a grain of justice. No pretence of kindness remained. The burning, red-hot coals of her eyes bored holes into Ruby. They delved deep with venom and something shrivelled inside her. Standing there, she felt alone and truly frightened.

"Peck her," came Cliona's voice, goading Goose on.

"Bring me my brush," repeated Granny G.

She spoke with absolute authority. Cliona crouched low and dipped her head in a fawning way.

Goose bent his long neck and, with difficulty, he took the brush in his beak.

"Good. Now give it to me."

With his head hanging down miserably, Goose waddled through the maze of flowerbeds. Twice, the brush became so cumbersome to him that he dropped it. Nudging it forwards on the ground was easier but slower. Granny G was not happy with this so, with a downcast expression, he picked it up and carried it in his beak again. Cliona clapped her hands with glee and laughed manically.

Stunned by their malice, Ruby hadn't moved but Cliona's delight was too much for her. Cliona reminded her of the nasty, gloating girls at school who always tried to be bigger by making someone else smaller. It made her blood boil.

Placing Dolph gently on the ground and kissing the top of his head, she said, "I'm sorry, Dolph."

Wincing as she jumped to her feet, she shouted as firmly as she could, "No! It's mine!"

"I don't think so," cackled Granny G. "Bring it, Goose!"

Breathless, Goose had paused in his task. His head flicked around to give Ruby a withering stare. As he did, a stone hit him squarely between the eyes. His legs buckled beneath him and he collapsed in an unmoving lump. The brush fell from his beak to the ground, landing with a clunk.

"I'll get it. Me!" Cliona raised a hand as she sprang forwards to retrieve it.

Granny G rubbed her hands together in anticipation and delight at Cliona's willingness. Yet a movement to the side of her made her turn reluctantly to catch sight of a mer boy, the particularly meddlesome one, grinning. His arms were behind his back as if he was hiding something. The rest of the children had left the garden and were standing on the other side of the wall. A sneer crossed her face.

Seeing Cliona set off spurred Ruby on. If it was a race, she intended to win. No way was she going to be beaten by Cliona. Scrambling and scurrying as fast as they could go, the two girls sprinted for the brush. Ruby's sore knees slowed her down and she saw that Cliona was gaining on her. A steely determination flooded her. This time, a spiteful girl was not about to get the better of her.

As the next flowerbed approached, she gave a mighty leap and jumped over it. Half rolling, she grabbed for the brush at the same moment as Cliona's outstretched hand touched it. Pulling on either side of it in a tug of war they gritted their teeth and glared at each other.

"Get off, squirt," Cliona yelled into Ruby's face.

"No, never," she retaliated.

Cliona went for Ruby's hair but, because of its shortness, failed to grab a good handful.

"Give it to me!" she shouted.

Ruby didn't waste her breath on words. Instead, she yanked hard on the brush. Cliona's hold weakened, leaving her sprawling on the ground. Clutching it to her, Ruby pushed herself up and away.

A cry of encouragement came from the watching children.

"Come on, Ruby," they screamed.

Cliona didn't give up that easily, though, and latched on to one of Ruby's legs. Hauling on it, Cliona tried to knock her off balance. Ruby managed to stay on her feet but however much she kicked, she couldn't escape.

Granny G came marching towards them both shouting, "Hold on, Cliona!"

Watching from a safe distance, Finn caught the appeal for help in Ruby's face and launched a stone at Cliona. It missed. Weighing the pebbles in his hand, he chose another, took aim and threw. This one was luckier. It clipped Cliona on the side of the head and cut her. A slow trickle of blood made its way down her cheek. Letting go of Ruby, she put an unbelieving hand up to her face and burst into tears.

"I hate you. You're so mean."

The words only grazed Ruby's back, though, because she hadn't hung around to listen. She raced as hard as she could for the gate. As it rattled behind her, she felt so relieved to be out of the garden and away from the house and Granny G. Sylvie passed Dolph to her. Ruby's face lit up with thanks into the warmest smile she had given for a long time.

Chapter 21

"Let's go, Ruby," Finn said, and this time Ruby wasn't waiting a second longer.

Carrying Dolph tenderly, she set off with the others.

"Make for the trees," said Zale, pointing towards the closest ones.

Limping and dragging their weary bodies, they trudged in silence. Fear prickled their skin so they each sneaked surreptitious glances behind, feeling sure that they were being followed. The only sound was Granny G's voice rising and falling as she berated Cliona. A howl of pain gave Ruby a start. Turning round, she saw Cliona crying pitifully as she clutched a hand, the one that had let go of Ruby, to her chest.

"Don't stop," urged the new boy, seeing her hesitate.

Soon the ruined house and its unfortunate inhabitants were out of sight.

The unrelenting rain had plastered their hair against their faces and they began shivering with the damp cold. The first trees provided some relief from the drizzle but their meagre spindles gave scant cover. Large raindrops fell from them, stinging the children's blue skin. At last, they happened upon a generous tree with wide-spreading branches and a bed of dry leaves under it. Throwing themselves down, they lay there, grateful for a moment of peace.

The new boy told them about himself. His name was Seager. His memories were hazy but he guessed that he had been buried in Granny G's flowerbed for many years. He spoke in a steady, matter-of-fact voice while holding the conch shell so tightly that his knuckles glowed white. His story seemed even sadder to Ruby for his gentle acceptance of his imprisonment. All day long, it had felt like a dusky evening but now Ruby realised that this seemingly endless day was truly fading.

Dolph lay on Ruby's lap where she inspected his small body for wounds. A gash ran along one side of his flank. He gave a whimper when her carefully exploring fingers found it. Ianthe crawled over to them and gently spread some of her sea urchin butter on it. Dolph whined before settling and letting his eyes close. Ruby curled around him and fell asleep instantly.

Waking with a start, she stretched and yawned uncontrollably as she sat up. Zale lay on his back, half propped against the tree. His mouth was open and Ruby squashed down a giggle at the thought of dropping something into it. The others were talking in serious, hushed voices which sobered her up quickly.

Seager's head rested on his knees while he twirled his conch shell between his hands. Round and round it went, the sole focus of his concentration.

"I must get back to the sea," he said. "I can feel it calling me."

"Me, too."

"Yes," came a soft rumbling of agreement.

"Can she get there before us without Goose?" questioned Finn. "We must leave now. We can't rest here any longer."

Seager stood up, shaking his limbs impatiently.

Ruby was still holding the brush. "I need to get my mirror back."

The quiet determination in her statement attracted everyone's attention. Their gaze was drawn to her brush.

"I came with a mirror and left it in a tree. I took the brush from Granny G. It matches my mirror. I don't know why I took it. I just did." She shrugged and stood up, brushing dirt from her trousers. "I'm not leaving without it."

"A tree?" said Finn, trying to catch up with all the details.

"Yes."

"Why?" said Finn, palms held upwards as three heads nodded in agreement.

"Why a tree? Why a mirror? Why leave it?" they all questioned her at once.

"I don't know. I don't know! Alright?" Ruby's mouth was set firm, daring them to challenge her further.

Finn stared at Ruby then down at the ground and sighed, "Well, where is this tree?"

"I'm not sure. I found it on my way to the cottage, the first evening. I've been searching for it ever since. Granny G wanted me to bring her a present so much and sent me out every day but I never did find it." Ruby's voice faded away.

Desperately suppressing a groan of frustration, Finn said, patiently, "There are trees all around, Ruby. I don't think that we are going to be able to find it."

"It was special. The trunk bends right over to make a doorway. I'll find it. I'm not going back without my mirror. You don't understand." Ruby clenched her jaw in determination.

"I must get back to the sea," insisted Seager, simply ignoring Ruby, Finn, and their talk of trees and mirrors.

Finn, Sylvie, and Ianthe exchanged glances to see if any of them had answers but greeted each other with shrugs and worried expressions. Their hearts were with Seager but their loyalty was to Ruby. Without her, they wouldn't be free and reunited with their own treasures.

"I think we should stick together," said Sylvie.

"We are safer as a group." Ianthe smiled gently at Ruby.

"I can't go without my mirror. Don't worry about me. You all go on and I'll find it on my own." Misunderstanding their intent, Ruby placed her hands on her hips, feet apart, radiating defiance.

"No," said Zale, rising nimbly. "The brush has proved its power in your hands. If you want your mirror, I will help you find it."

"If Granny G thinks it is so valuable then we could be in great danger if we find it," said Sylvie.

"Do you think that is why she let us go?" asked Ianthe, nervously.

"It could help us," said Zale.

"Okay, we'll have to sort that out once we find it. But I think we should go now. Where to Ruby?" Finn rose with an easy grace as he spoke.

"I'm not sure. Let me think. Dusk was falling. The cottage was shiny and I had been following it. Dolph came, too. There were five silver trees in a circle and a bubble of water," Ruby spoke, pausing between statements as she tried to remember her first day on the land.

"Great," said Seager, sounding both downcast and impatient.

He folded his arms and scrutinised the horizon. Finn glared at him and put his arm around Ruby's shoulders.

"Okay, we'd better start searching for it."

Ruby gazed at him. In spite of everything, warmth spread through her. She belonged. Her spirits lifted, filling her with hope.

"Thank you for rescuing us, Ruby," Ianthe said, rising to stand beside her.

"I don't understand how come you have two treasures," said Seager, drawn into the plan despite his overwhelming longing for the sea.

"Explain as we go but we must move off now. Which way, Ruby?" Sylvie asked.

"Not without Dolph," said Ruby, as she bent to pick him up.

At the sound of his name he stirred, giving Ruby a doleful look of love with liquid brown eyes. Unfolding his body, he stretched his front legs out before having a good shake. Ignoring them all, he set off at a trot, pausing only to check over his shoulder that they were following. When he saw they weren't, he barked as if to say, "What are you waiting for?" then went on. Every one of them burst out laughing. Without wasting another minute in case he disappeared, they scuttled after him.

Dolph kept up a steady pace and they jogged along to keep up with him. With their fear less immediate, they skipped and ran and danced. Their joy at being out in the world, alive and no longer captive to Granny G, bubbled up. They tumbled over one another with questions for Ruby. How had she got two treasures? What had made her leave one of them in a tree? Running between and through their search for answers lay the most important point of all. If Ruby's journey had been like theirs then they would never have escaped. Ruby told them the story of her arrival and how she found the cottage. She wasn't able to explain why she had hidden her mirror and was still slightly bemused.

While they rested under the great tree, the clouds were swept aside. Sitting low in the sky sat the fat, white moon, touching everything with its ghostly light. Wet ferns brushed against their legs as they pushed a path through the vegetation. Large drops of rain rolled off leaves to plop heavily on their heads as they made their way. Curling tendrils of steam rose up mistily from the damp ground. Their exuberance faded and they slowed to a steady, rhythmic walk as they spread out in a straggly line.

Seager was able to stride ahead with his long, strong legs while petite Ianthe lagged behind. At one point, they lost sight of the whole group in the fog. Finn called to Seager to let them all catch up but the murk swallowed up his voice. Once Seager re-emerged from the haze, they promised to stay together. Seager struggled to go at their pace. Every inch of his large being was poised to run, pell-mell, in the direction of the sea. Sticking close wasn't as fast but was more companionable and they told each other stories as they travelled.

Becoming weary, their footsteps dragged and their spirits plummeted. Seager spoke aloud the secret thought which silently nagged at them. "I hope Dolph knows where he's going."

"Look over there. That's it. I'm sure it is!" Ruby's voice squeaked with relief as she pointed. "It is, it is! I remember. Those are the five silver trees. Let's go! Dolph, I'm coming."

Leaping over the undergrowth, Ruby shot off towards the trees. Happiness welled up in her. She ran as if her younger, more carefree self was still in the glade; as if she could recapture her innocence.

Spurred on by Ruby's enthusiasm, everyone bounded forwards. Dolph was first into the clearing with Ruby on his tail. It really was the same place. Ruby felt as if she was greeting an old friend with that wonderful mixture of treasured memories and the expectation of new ones to come. The arched tree with its branches shooting out remained at the centre with the blue flowers still swinging their heads as if chatting prettily. The spring of refreshing, life-giving water bubbled. Scooping water up in her hands, Ruby had a deep, thirst-quenching drink. When Finn and the others caught up with her, they all drank greedily.

Feeling light as if a weight had lifted, Ruby skipped around the glade. Ianthe and Sylvie joined her and, holding hands, they leapt about. Seager lay amongst the blue flowers and rolled onto his tummy.

"It's good here," he stated, in his flat way.

Finn laughed. "Is your mirror here, Ruby?"

"Yes, it must be. I left it in the trunk of the tree. It's hollow, you know."

Together, they wandered over to inspect the tree. In the raggedy moonlight, nothing was easy to figure out. Ruby was about to show him where she had climbed up to find the hollow inside when a rustling in the leaves made them both freeze. A pale hand, wrinkled and liver-spotted, crept round the trunk, followed by an old lady whose grey hair fell to her feet. Her face was crinkly with kindness, with two intelligent yet sad eyes gazing out. Her tones were so low that Ruby strained to hear her.

"Ruby?"

"Stay back!" shouted Finn.

Zale, Seager, Ianthe, and Sylvie all stopped what they were doing at the sound of his voice. The old woman came out from behind the tree, holding her hands up passively.

"Nan?" questioned Ruby.

Unable to believe the sight in front of her, she stood there, open-mouthed.

"Ruby," said her Nan again, warmth and tenderness oozing from every syllable.

Finn relaxed his stance, softening his face, bemused.

"It's my Nan."

Ruby's face shone at everyone, flushed pink, tears glistening on her cheeks like a dewy apple.

Enclosing Nan in her arms, she almost picked her up off the ground and sang, "Nan, Nan, my Nan."

Neither Ruby nor Nan understood why the other happened to be there or what miracle had brought them together. By now, everyone had become curious. They figured out that something amazing was going on. Ruby and Nan's delight at being reunited was infectious and soon they were all wreathed in smiles. Arms circling waists, Ruby and Nan joined the others to sit close to the tree.

"Nan was missing, weren't you?"

Nan nodded.

"Everyone thought she had gone forever," Ruby explained, "but I didn't." Ruby raised her eyes to Nan's. "I never did. I knew you would come back."

Nan took Ruby's hand and held it between her own two warm ones.

"These are my friends, Nan."

As Ruby said it, she knew it to be true and a rush of emotion flashed through her. After introducing them all, Nan spoke.

"I owe Ruby my life," she said. "Without her faith I would be trapped here forever."

Finn added, "Without Ruby, we would all be trapped here on the land."

"I will tell you all my story," continued Nan. "Many, many years ago, my family were Healers and we were given a brush and mirror made from narwhal horn as a gift from the sea unicorns. They were said to have magical properties that protected their owners. The witch who lives in yonder cottage stole the brush when she was a young girl. We did not know what she would become. Since then, life has not gone well for us Healers. I came here to ask her to return it of her own free will. I did not believe that she would but it was my only hope to give the Healers back their powers. Tragically, bitterness and a desire for revenge have wiped out any good that was in her. My visit did not go well. On my journey back to the sea, she followed me and beat me sorely. She left me for dead. I had a little strength still and managed to crawl here for shelter. This rowan tree folded me into itself so I could be healed and it suffered greatly for its generosity." Nan stroked the trunk tenderly.

"Ruby," Nan turned to her granddaughter, "when you left the mirror with me, I began to regain my energy until the day came when I took my own form again. For the moment, we are well guarded here. These trees will hide us from her, just as they have hidden and protected me."

"No wonder there is such peace," said Ruby, full of wonder.

"As long as she has the narwhal handle brush, we are all still in great danger," Nan added, directly meeting the earnest gazes studying her. "Once we leave here, who knows … ?"

"Nan …" Ruby withdrew the brush from her bag and placed it in Nan's hands. "Here you are."

"What? How, Ruby?" Nan was flabbergasted.

"I stumbled upon it. Sort of by accident. Somehow I knew it belonged to us and I kept it. I stole it! But as soon as I held it, it spoke to me. It gave me courage. The handle was cool and pure."

Blurting this out with a tinge of guilt, Ruby shrugged. She wasn't quite comfortable with the way she had come by it.

Ianthe spoke up. "Finn rescued my urchin shell for me."

One by one, they revealed their own treasures.

"Well, I never," said Nan, ashen-faced at what she saw. "You are all Healers. The next generation of mer needs you."

Left unspoken was how they would get back to their ocean homes safely.

"Does Granny G, the witch, not have power anymore?" ventured Sylvie.

"Oh, no. She is ancient and has been learning and perfecting her craft for a vast number of years. With your treasures, her power would have been greater than any witch who came before her. She is still a force to be reckoned with." With this thought, Nan shrank back into herself and fell quiet.

Ruby put her arms around her and they sat there peacefully. Dolph curled up on Ruby's lap with his head on his paws. His tail thumped happily against Ruby's thigh.

Anxiety creased a small furrow in Sylvie's brow as she beckoned to Finn and the others. Treading softly, they crossed the glade.

"Nan looks very weak," Sylvie said, sounding worried, "but I don't think Ruby can see it."

"She will have to come with us," added Finn. "Nobody is to be left in this place."

"She will slow us down even more," said Seager, pounding his heart with his fist. "I dream of my home."

"We have to stick together," said Zale.

"I was the first to make my way to this land. Life stopped for me and the days became endless, without hope." Seager's face was stricken with misery.

Leaning into him, Ianthe placed a tender hand on his arm. "She isn't here yet. Goose was injured and she might not be able to fly for a while. We will all get out of here."

"Yes, you are right. I do know it. It's just ... Okay, Zale. We'll have to carry her."

"I really don't think Ruby understands how weak Nan is," said Sylvie, almost to herself.

It did not take them long to say their goodbyes to the kind rowan tree and gentle glade. With Nan on Seager's back, they left the haven of the clearing, heading for the bay, the sea, and whatever else might come. With their spirits restored, the threat of Granny G had faded.

"We'll get home easily now," hummed Ruby to herself as she walked along.

Chapter 22

The night sky remained mostly crystal clear with wispy clouds scudding across it, playing peek-a-boo with the bright stars and luminous moon. Without the moon's reassuring light, Ruby couldn't see her hand in front of her face and was forced to stop and wait until the cloud hurried on its way. The track back to the bay was as densely obscure as she remembered it. Thick foliage slowed their going to a sea snail's pace. Wiping her brow with her hand, Ruby sighed. Already it seemed an age since her refreshing drink from the bubble of water.

In single file, they stuck rigidly to the trail mapped out by Dolph. Finn went first, bashing at some of the thorny plants with a stick to clear a path. Seager and Zale came last, taking it in turns to support Nan. They were too heavily burdened to speak. Whichever of them was carrying her had his face set hard and would pause now and then to adjust the position he was holding her in before setting off anew. In the beginning, she had felt like a tiny, bony bird, however the longer they carried her, the more of a dead weight she became. Relief lightened their features when it was time to pass her over. Nan barely stirred in her slumbers when they transferred her, after which she settled to sleep again with her head resting on either of the boys' shoulders.

Their anxiety about what lay ahead diminished as they took one step and then the next, the arduous trek demanding all their concentration. Each of them sank quietly into their own journey except for Sylvie and Ianthe, who were able to rise above the moment. Hand in hand, they moved in harmony, speaking so softly their voices could have been mistaken for the breeze rustling the leaves overhead. Once, Ianthe gave a skittish jump and a wail that she quickly silenced by stuffing her hand in her mouth. Pointing to the dark outline of a shrub she explained, with a nervous laugh, how she had imagined it was Granny G. After that, they were all more alert.

Sylvie kept a look out at the tree line, afraid that Granny G would swoop on them, astride Goose. Past and future dangers faded for Ruby as her mind centred on Nan and the miracle of the present moment. She hugged her happiness at finding Nan to herself. Her whole family had believed Nan gone forever, except for her. She had refused to accept it as the truth and now she, Ruby, had found Nan and was taking her home, helped by a group of friends. A few days ago, it had been unimaginable. Deep in her own thoughts, she barely noticed where she placed her feet or her surroundings.

At last, the land opened up and they fanned out to walk side by side. Sooner than they expected, they arrived at the cliff top path that descended to the bay below. A mirror moon rippled on the waves enticingly. By now, they were a heady brew of nerves and excitement. None of them had glimpsed their salty home in an age and they stood there, drinking in the view and gulping lungfuls of sea air.

Seager swelled with well-being. His shoulders drew back, his chin lifted; he grew as if shrugging off the burden of his captivity. He shook his hair and stomped the ground like a wild stallion about to gallop away. Already a head taller than everyone else, he appeared to Ruby to be a giant. Zale seemed to have shrunk with the effort of carrying Nan. As soon as they stopped, he sank to his knees, relieving himself of her weight.

With mixed emotions, Ruby looked at the bay, the place where she spent those playful hours learning to walk, where her adventures began. That innocent and carefree time seemed to belong to a much younger girl. She gave an involuntary shudder. Was she really the same person? And yet ... part of her had been bowed down and so lonely. Her mixed feelings were reflected in the faces of the others, her allies. Seager's impatience broke into her memories with a snort of agitation.

"Slowly," said Ianthe. "Granny G will not let us go without a fight. We have been lucky so far."

"Do we have a plan?" asked Finn, turning to Sylvie.

"Stay together," she replied.

"Together," Zale repeated, with a grimness in his sharp-toothed smile. "Let's go."

Throughout this discussion, Ruby had been sitting beside Nan, who was only half awake.

"Thank you for bringing her on your backs," she said to Seager and Zale.

She patted her bag where the mirror and brush were.

"We have to try, don't we," she said, twisting a fingernail between her teeth.

159

"Come," said Seager, giving her his hand to pull her up, before lifting Nan.

Once he had Nan settled, he started to sing. His voice cut through the cool night air, pure and true. It was an ancient mer ballad. The words were in an old mer dialect, no longer spoken. After the second line, Ianthe joined in, her sweet, high notes complimenting Seager's deeper ones. As they sang on, Finn, Sylvie, and Zale harmonised with the other two. Ruby was freshly astonished. Nan had taught this ballad to her and they had sung while exploring together. She had never heard it sung by anyone else in her life. None of the children at school knew it. Raising her own voice, she let herself be carried up and away with the music.

As the last note faded, a quiet descended so deep it seemed as if even the smallest animal had been listening and was still holding its breath in rapture. Nan lifted her head from Seager's shoulder.

"It is the Healers song. The words bring hope. You are all the missing Healers' children. No one else would know it."

Then, in her quavering, old-lady soprano, she started the song again. As she wobbled on a high note, Seager's deep tones boomed in, adding strength to hers. Walking and beating out the rhythm of the music gave them a surge of confidence. Stepping lightly with her head held up, Ruby linked arms with Finn. Faster than they could have imagined, they arrived on the shingle, two by two.

The sand shone silver in the moonlight, lapped by blue-black wavelets. Home at last.

"Nan, we're almost there," Ruby cried.

Her longing to dip her head under the swell and to feel the push of it against her skin made her so dizzy she stretched out her arms towards it, everyone and everything forgotten in her all-consuming desire.

Chapter 23

A cackling laugh bounced off the cliff walls edging the cove.

"Welcome, welcome!"

It echoed like a hundred witches calling from every crack and crevice, every tree and branch, an enchantment of them ready to plummet out of the sky. Ruby ducked, covering her head with her hands. Her eyes were as round as saucers. The confidence and courage that she had sung into her heart walking along the clifftop fled. The small band of children backed against each other in a chaotic clump. Gasps of shock and whimpers of confusion came from them. Nan hid behind Seager, not wanting her presence to be discovered.

Peering through the lattice of her fingers, Ruby scanned the beach. In the middle of it sat an armchair! Staring, she could just make out that it was Granny G's wing-backed armchair. Ruby blinked with disbelief then she began to quake. Seeing such an ordinary household object here somehow felt ominous. How could Granny G be relaxing in her armchair while waiting for them? Around the edge of the chair appeared a hand holding a baton and protruding under it, a pair of glitter shoes were lapped by the tide. Granny G knew exactly when they had arrived without even bothering to turn her head in their direction. As the last echo died away, the baton slowly came to rest on her knees. It seemed to Ruby as if Granny G was the conductor of an orchestra of discordant, braying witches.

So mesmerised had she been by Granny G that it took her a minute to notice that Cliona was crouched the other side of the chair. She was absorbed with drawing patterns with a stick in the sand. Goose looked in a sorry state with all the stuffing knocked out of him. His head hung low and the once shiny black of his feathers was now dull.

"At least I'm not alone anymore," thought Ruby, aware of her friends close beside her.

"Shuffle," said Sylvie, so silently that Ruby wasn't sure what she had said or meant, except for a tug on her sleeve.

Sylvie took tiny, mincing steps towards the dark water. Giving them all an intense, meaningful glance she beckoned them to follow her. Urgent hissing came from her like air escaping from a balloon while her fingers gesticulated wildly.

"Where are you going?" Ruby's cry was hushed with fear but her confusion was clear.

In a matter of seconds, Sylvie was at least five paces in front of them. Nobody else knew quite what to do. From being still and tightly-packed, they became agitated, moving from foot to foot and half reaching to her, only to withdraw into themselves again.

"Stay. Stay," Ruby urged.

Out of the corner of her eye, she thought she saw Granny G's foot begin to beat faster. Finn nodded at her but was torn between staying and rescuing Sylvie. In a half crouch, he loped after her. With her loyalties divided, Ianthe tiptoed in their direction. Her movements were so light, Ruby had the impression that she was pretending to be invisible. Their tight huddle broken, they were now strung out like fence posts along the sand. Only Zale and Seager, who were busy swapping Nan over, remained.

To add to Ruby's distress, Dolph chose this moment to disappear into the scrubland. She lunged for the scruff of his neck but failed to grab it, losing her balance and sprawling on the sand. Regaining her footing, Ruby could see that Sylvie was now a dark shape, she had covered so much ground so fast. Part of her was willing Sylvie on; to run, run for the sea, home, and safety while another part was couched in sadness and dread that their comradeship had dissolved so quickly. She struggled to believe it.

"Together," Nan had said.

It had seemed like a simple thing to do and they had agreed wholeheartedly as they strode out. Nodding their heads, they had repeated the word, feeling its strength and solidarity. Yet, within minutes, Granny G had set fear into every one of their hearts which had forced them apart.

Turning to Zale and Seager, on the point of repeating the catchphrase, "Let's stay together,'" her words faded because neither of them heard her. They were so wrapped up in their own desires they were deaf to anything else.

Seager's body was poised to run and catch up with Sylvie on her wild dash to the ocean while Zale cowered as the witches started a fresh invocation. Ruby couldn't understand the words but their evil intent was crystal clear. Granny G had risen from her armchair to wave her baton at the beach. Her chin was held high as she crooned. Quivering at her feet, her silhouette resembled a vengeful crow. Her chant was picked up by the circle of witches and resounded over and over until it blended into a deafening crescendo of noise. Peering behind her along the top of the cliffs, Ruby wanted to see how many of them there were. She stared until her eyes smarted. The moonlight created eerie shadows but there was no movement. They sounded so real yet there was nothing there. Ruby's mind felt sluggish and slow as it dawned on her that she was hearing an echo of Granny G.

"What about the others?" she thought.

Sylvie had risen from her crab-like motion to run full pelt into the sea when she stumbled. Thrown off balance, Sylvie's arms swayed about as if they were the branches of a tree in a storm. Her screams cut through the echo-witches' hymn. Sand was rushing towards her and eddying about her legs so that she was planted in the ground. Ruby gasped. The sand cloud was unstoppable and rapidly covered Sylvie's feet before inching up her legs. Believing she was going to be buried again, Sylvie struggled against it, frightened for her life.

Bent double, Finn was fighting to get to her. A strong wind had whipped itself into a frenzy and was forcing him back. Cupping his hands around his mouth, he shouted at her. The wind seized his words and carried them off. Ruby caught them as they flew past, "The coral! Use the coral!"

As if in a dream, Sylvie steadied. Somehow, she must have heard his cry. She cradled the coral in her hands and dropped her chin so that she could hold it in her gaze. Concentrating hard, she stared at it and to Ruby's amazement, the tide rushed towards Sylvie. By now, the sand had reached the top of her thighs and Sylvie's single-mindedness collapsed. Her terror resurfaced. She turned her face in Ruby's direction, the whites of her eyes visible, her face alive with panic. Ruby felt completely helpless as she watched but then she saw Sylvie return her attention to the coral with a supreme effort of will. Ruby unclenched her hands.

Up crept the tide, closer and closer, and as it came, it sucked the sand away. A pool formed around her legs, getting deeper and releasing them from the sand's grip, as Sylvie focused on her coral. The wind dropped, allowing Finn and Ianthe to splash into the oncoming seawater. Once free, Sylvie threw herself down with Finn and Ianthe so that the three of them were dragged into the depths of the retreating water where the open sea waited to embrace them. Ruby heard a great "whoop" of delight from Finn.

It was too much for Seager. His face twisted in an agony of longing. Without a second thought, he took huge strides to Sylvie's ebbing pool, catching the tail end of it and disappearing with the others. Carrying Nan stopped Zale from being able to follow. His eyes were fixed only on the shining, black waves. He moaned and Nan slipped from his grasp onto the ground.

"Nan!" screamed Ruby.

Alarmed by her anguish, Zale was drawn back to her plight. Nan tried to speak but her voice croaked, dry and hoarse. Ruby and Zale leant in close to hear her.

"We have failed," she said. "She has tricked them."

Exhausted, Nan shut her eyes.

"There must be something we can do. There just must," said Ruby.

She clasped her hand around the handle of the mirror, wishing with all her might.

"Whoa, look at the storm," said Zale.

On the horizon, castles of billowing cloud were growing, each trying to outstrip the others in glory, as they towered higher and higher until it seemed they must topple over. Adding to their awesome majesty, lightning zipped through them in streaks of purple, orange, and blue. The echoes of the cackling witches stopped and an expectant hush settled on the cove. Ruby held her breath as she waited, the tiny hairs on the back of her neck raised in anticipation. A clap of thunder, followed swiftly by another, sent their world into turmoil again.

Standing, with one arm Granny G beckoned the storm onwards, with the other she appeared to be stirring an invisible pot. Ruby watched her as if hypnotised. Slowly, her attention was drawn to the water in the bay which was churning and swirling as if it was being rolled about in an enormous cauldron. Round and round it went, faster and faster, forming a vortex in the middle that sucked air towards it and created a spinning bank of water. Caught on its edges were Seager, Finn, Sylvie, and Ianthe. Their heads bobbed on the lip of the wall and their arms waved in desperation. Ruby became dizzy as she tried to keep them in sight. Then they must have gone under and she saw them no more.

She had heard tales of mer who were drawn into maelstroms but nothing in her imagination had prepared her for this. The force of the water as it spun around the whirlpool's centre was jaw-dropping. Debris was thrown against the rocks on the outside. It was impossible to believe that anything could escape. Mouth agape, she saw that her friends were helpless against this force and were in grave danger. She squashed down the thought, "if they are still alive". Now Ruby knew what Nan had meant. The sea had been a mirage of safety, another trap.

Chapter 24

Nan lay next to Zale, hardly moving. Ruby stroked her hair off her face. Still holding the mirror by its handle, she crouched close to Zale, using her body to protect Nan.

"Zale," she said, "we mustn't give up yet."

For a moment, she thought he hadn't heard her but then he turned with his usual sharky smile on his face. Her relief lasted an instant before she realised that this time there was no mischief in it because it didn't reach his eyes.

"No, Ruby," he replied.

Crackles of energy darted about Granny G as she whipped up her evil spell to greater heights. Cliona had broken from her squatting position and was leaping and cavorting on the water's edge, throwing handfuls of sea upwards to fall like tears around her. Ruby could hear her manic laughter. She appeared to be a wild thing, possessed by an uncontrollable madness. Goose had woken from his slump and uttered a pathetic "ahh-honk," or at least Ruby saw him raise his neck as if calling. His voice was drowned out by the general cacophony surrounding them.

A heavy drop of rain landed on Ruby's head. At first, it fell in slow, fat blobs; then it pelted heavily down. The storm was on top of them now, and fiercer than ever. The thunder was deafening and the lightning zigzagged out of the sky. Zale gesticulated towards a huddle of trees a short distance away which offered some shelter. Then he moved to pick up Nan who still lay inert. Ruby's vision blurred and she wasn't sure if it was the water running across her cheeks in rivulets or tears because of Zale's kindness in not deserting her. She cast her head away and blinked hard.

The rain was so dense that the bay and Granny G were no longer clearly visible. Rain soaked their faces and plastered their hair to their heads. Ruby nodded and half rose when a ball of lightning raced out of the sky, hitting the trees. Flames licked up them, stripping them of their greenery, turning them to blackened stumps. Both Ruby and Zale staggered on the sand.

"Stay down!" shouted Ruby.

Another streak of electricity hit the beach further along, leaving an amber burning bush as the only bright colour in the rain-soaked desolation of the night. For a second, the rain thinned, giving Ruby a window through which she spotted Granny G whose arms were raised to the heavens, snaking a dance of destruction.

Granny G's face was aglow. The excitement poured off her. She shone energy; radiated joy. Amongst the horror, the grappling for life which the rest of them were battling, she exuded delight in the havoc she was creating. Ruby was mesmerised.

Behind her, Zale's whole demeanour slumped; with his arms clutching his knees, he rocked slightly, oozing despair. Nan lay as if dead. They had escaped one trap only to be caught in another and this time, there was nowhere to run to. How could they get out of this?

But still Ruby could not draw her gaze from Granny G. Cliona and Goose seemed to be revitalised by being so close to her. Cliona stood tall with her head held high and Goose's tail feathers wagged from side to side with eager flicks. Granny G laughed and the sound was a pure musical note of pleasure, not the hint of a cackle in it.

A steady stream of water dripped from Ruby's nose and chin. The ends of her hair were a waterfall, her feet were mired in the sticky sand but she did not stop staring. She twisted her bag around her body until it was lying in the cup of her hands in front of her. The bulky shapes of the brush and mirror were too big to fit snugly and fell from her grasp. Freed from the bag, they sprawled at Ruby's feet. The mirror lay upon its back, reflecting the wild sky. Scrabbling for them, Ruby felt an unnatural quiet descend.

Nothing else had drawn Granny G's attention away from her conducting of the storm but this did. When she saw Ruby, bedraggled and almost alone, a smile of satisfaction spread over her face but Ruby did not turn away. Holding Granny G's face eye to eye, she stood up straight and proud. With the slightest movement of her fingers, Granny G summoned something towards her. An enormous flash of lightning ripped through the furious clouds, searching for a place to reach earth. For a fraction of a second, not really long enough for the thought to form, Ruby was sure it was coming for her. All she could see was a superior smirk curling the edges of Granny G's mouth. Standing her ground, she held the mirror against her heart, one of the last survivors of the Healers. She knew that if this was it, there was nothing she could do anymore.

At the last second, the lightning twisted in its path and instead found a home in Granny G's outstretched arms. For a second, it played with her, transforming her into a rag doll, her arms and legs jerking unnaturally before it sank into the sand.

Ruby's knees gave way and Zale pulled her close to him.

"Shhh," he soothed, over and over again as she shook uncontrollably.

They lay locked around each other, not daring to move. No more lightning came. The rain eased. The threatening clouds rolled back and the sky cleared, revealing patches of early morning light, spots of blue hope. The sea calmed, making a mockery of its former agitation.

"Ruby," said a voice.

Sitting up was Nan, She appeared small and fragile but strong enough to ask questions.

"How did you do that? I thought we were doomed."

"Me?" replied Ruby, "I didn't do anything. The storm got her."

"Hmmm," was all Nan said.

"It was you, Ruby!" Zale said, giving her a big hug. "She was really brave, Nan."

"The mirror!" Ruby said, and showed it to them.

Running down the centre of it was a crack cutting it forever into two parts.

"That's what did it!"

Zale and Nan exchanged glances with a slight shrug. Then Zale jumped up, saying,

"Let's go home."

"Why didn't I think of that?" laughed Ruby.

Zale helped Nan up as the sun touched the horizon, a sign of bright light highlighting the new morning. Dolph bounded out of the scrubland and barked and barked at them. As he flew across the sand towards her, Ruby remembered how she had been afraid of him on that first day. Since then, he had become her best friend. Patting her thighs, she called him to her. He came at a trot, almost bowling her over before placing his two front paws on her legs and giving her his most entreating look. His thick tail thumped happily. Tears of sadness wet her face as she kissed the top of his head and rubbed both his ears in her hands.

"I'll miss you so much."

He licked her face.

"Eww, Dolph," she laughed.

Looking pleadingly up at Nan and Zale, she said, "Dolph will be alone if we all go."

Rising, she chewed her lip, "How can I leave him? We wouldn't be free without his help."

On shaky legs, Nan took Ruby's face in her hands. "Ruby, Dolph is the guardian of the bay. He did what he had to do and did it gladly, for he loves you."

As if in reply, Dolph went, "Yip, yip."

Nan continued, "He will be able to live free and happy now. You have given him that."

Zale, then Nan, said their goodbyes to Dolph.

"Thank you, Dolph, for everything," whispered Ruby.

With a final "Yip," Dolph scampered back the way he had come to the scrubland. Ruby watched him go, staring after him until his last paw was out of sight.

"Ready?" asked Nan, gently.

"Yes," replied Ruby. "It's time."

"What's that?" demanded Zale, pointing.

Standing beside the now-forlorn armchair where Granny G had stood was a shining, glass statue.

"It is a warning to all who come here," said Nan, gravely. "The lightning has turned her to glass."

At the foot of the statue was a pitiful creature, sobbing. It was Cliona.

"Zale?" asked Ruby.

"We can't do anything for her," he told her. "Come, it is time to go home."

Out in the bay, four shapes were riding up and down on the waves.

"I'm coming," said Zale.

He took off at full pelt, running at the water with childish enthusiasm, arms and legs splashing wildly.

Nan followed, slipping in more slowly as the sea gently engulfed her. When their heads had disappeared beneath the foam, Ruby took a last look at the bay. The thin light of morning was creeping in, wiping away the events of the night and touching the bay with new promise. Wading in until her feet lifted, she dived down before swimming out to meet her friends. For the first few strokes, she still had her clumsy, ungainly legs then her tail reformed. It was a beautiful miracle to swim with a well-muscled tail propelling her along. Her delight at being mer and back in her ocean home had her twisting, somersaulting, and playing in the water.

Finn arrived and executed a perfect dolphin mid-air spin.

"Show off," she teased, remembering Eric and the way he liked to prance and preen in front of her.

Her old worries seemed so small after everything that had happened.

"Home, Mum, Dad, and Eric," she said happily, then added, "with Nan."

She punched the air with joy.

"What will you tell them?" asked Finn, bobbing beside her.

"The truth of course," replied Ruby.

"The truth? You'll be asking for trouble. We'd better come with you."

"Trouble? Me? Asking for trouble? Not anymore." Laughing, she shouted, "Tig! Bet you can't catch me!"

Then she plunged into the deep and was gone.

When Moira Cormack was a child, her family moved house all the time so she made a secret world for herself in books. She hid everywhere and anywhere in order to read. By the time her family eventually settled, her habit of hiding in books was well-established and one she has never let go of.

After completing a degree in Philosophy, Moira worked in France for a couple of years before settling down to a career in London. She now lives just outside Edinburgh, very near where she first started life, with her four daughters, dog, and two cats. As well as running round after her daughters, she takes parenting classes for a living.

Moira loves walking her dog beside the river every day. Ruby's story unfolded for her while she walked. She has always written and doesn't know why it took her so long to write a book. She says, "It has been an inspiring, magical experience, like finding I'm home at last."

'The Witch of Land and Sea' is her first novel.